TAGGER
Alone Along the Mystic River

by
J. A. Louthain

Illustrated by Andrea Eberbach

Alexie Books
Carmel, Indiana

Tagger

Alexie Books
A Division of Alexie Enterprises, Inc.
P.O. Box 3843
Carmel, IN 46082

ISBN 0-9679416-0-1

Printed and bound in the United States of America

Dedication

This book is dedicated to my loving father, the late Edward Anderson, who changed my life with a little bedtime story, so many years ago; to my late mother, Judy Anderson who taught me to strive for more; to my dear friend Diane Risch, who left this life before she could read the story; and to my awesome husband, Ronald, who suffered with me as I wrote and rewrote the words that meant so much to me.

I would also like to thank William Peterson, Senior Curator, at Mystic Seaport and Wendy Schnur, librarian, at the Museum of America and the Sea at Mystic, Connecticut. Their assistance was invaluable, because of their extensive knowledge of the Mystic River area.

Chapter One
The Storm

The thunder boomed above her and seemed to shake the very earth beneath her feet. It sounded like a giant potato wagon in the sky, rumbling loose down a hill and scattering its lumpy load.

The girl quickened her pace as the large raindrops pelted her head and shoulders. Her clothes didn't provide much protection against the downpour.

She wore patched cotton britches, an old white muslin shirt, with three buttons at the top and a black, bulky cloak. Strange garb for a little girl! And a strange name! As of this day she would call herself "Tagger," a name she picked for herself, because she was often laughed at for tagging after people and asking questions. Prior to today she had been known as "Lizzie," just Lizzie. It had been so long since she had heard her last name that she had forgotten it.

The rain ran in rivulets off her misshapen felt hat. Tagger was wet and scared. She was just trying to get home, but to a home she could barely remember. This dirt path with the sign pointing to Mystic Bridge seemed familiar enough, even in the darkening gloom of the storm, but she couldn't recall for sure.

The year was 1828 and Mystic Bridge was a flourishing New England fishing and shipbuilding village located in the southeast corner of the state of Connecticut. It was a quaint town, with one and a half or two story clapboard houses and shops, set on the east bank of the Mystic River. Tagger hadn't reached Mystic Bridge yet; she was still on the west side of the Mystic River between Noank and Portersville.

Life wasn't easy here along the river. The residents worked hard and relied heavily upon the sea for their income. Tall ships and whalers left often from the wooden wharf, plowing down the Mystic River and out to Fishers Island Sound. Local companies funded these expeditions which hunted seals and whales. Many valuable products were extracted from these creatures: warm skins for coats and hats from the seals and whale oil and whalebone from the massive whales. Hunting seals and whales was hard work and required courageous, weathered sailors to endure the elements for long periods of time.

Smaller fishing boats plied the waters as well, operated mostly by small crews or independent, local fishermen. These were hardy fellows too. They spent long days fishing in the sound and the open waters beyond for flounder, striped bass, bluefish, cod, oysters, lobsters and halibut. Much of the food fish caught by the independent fishermen fed their families throughout the year. If you lived along the Mystic River and didn't like seafood, you were mostly out of luck.

It was a busy area during the warmer months of the year, but when the winter nor'easters swept down from Canada, everything changed. Life became more challenging, and it was sometimes difficult for the villagers to even eke out a living.

But Tagger didn't know all of this. She was just a scared little girl, trying to find her old home and some relief from the summer storm.

The rain was coming in torrents now, making it nearly impossible for her to see the path. She thought about stopping, maybe hiding under a tree until the worst of the storm passed, but she knew she had to keep moving. She felt safer on the path; after all, she didn't know what might lurk in the storm-tangled woods by the side of the road.

Surely the rain would let up soon.

The wind swooshed behind her, propelling her even faster down the path. She was at a dead run now, but didn't really know where she was running. She was looking for a warm place where someone would take care of her—maybe fix her broth—tell her she was safe now.

Someone here had done that once—a kind, older lady with gray hair and a sunny smile. The girl had called her Nana. The kind lady had kept her warm and dry, fed her, sheltered her from the storms, held her hand when she was sick—but it was so long ago. She thought the lady must have been her grandmother. Would the lady remember her now, even if she found her? It had been years since she'd last seen her, Tagger thought.

She remembered only a little about her mother, Becky. She had always seemed so sad and distant. She wasn't mean to her daughter exactly; she just didn't seem to have much interest in caring for her.

Tagger did remember one incident about her mother— quite well. It had started on an overcast, late autumn day some four years past—back when she was known as Lizzie. It was one of those days when all she'd wanted to do was stay in bed and cuddle under her soft pink quilt, the one with the tiny embroidered strawberries. But instead her mother had wakened her early, shaking her shoulder and whispering firmly, "Get up, Lizzie, get up right now!"

When she started to protest sleepily, Becky would have none of it. "Be quiet, and do as I tell you."

Then in an authoritative manner that allowed for no nonsense, her mother dressed her quickly. Lizzie was surprised to see that Becky was shoving her into her best frilly dress—the one with the green sash. This was the dress she wore only for special occasions.

"What's wrong?" she whimpered. "Why are we hurrying so? Where are we going? Is Nana coming with us?" But there was no reply. She stared at her mother with big, sleepy eyes.

Without even saying goodbye to the kind older lady, who was still sleeping in the back bedroom, her mother steered her quickly out the front door, shutting it quietly behind them. A horse-drawn coach stood waiting in the gloom of the early morning.

"Please tell me where we're going, Momma," she begged pitifully, rubbing her eyes to force the sleep away.

Her mother stared at her for a moment, seemingly lost in her own thoughts. "We're going to Groton," she said simply.

"Aren't we going to say goodbye to Nana?" Lizzie asked, indignant that the older woman had been forgotten.

"No, we won't be waking her now," her mother said in a low whisper. "Come now, put on your cloak, and be quick with you. The coachman is waiting for us."

The confused girl could still remember the clippety-clop of the big roan horses as they set off on their journey. The stamping and whinnying of the huge beasts had frightened her at first, but soon she got used to the rhythmic pace they set.

The trip seemed to last forever, because she had never been this far away from home before. Suddenly the coach driver stopped the big horses, and Lizzie saw they had neared an unusual wooden bridge over a large body of water.

"Need some money for the drawbridge," the coachman boomed as he stuck his head into the window next to her mother.

"How much?" Becky asked quietly.

"Twenty-five cents for a coach," he replied without hesitation, obviously familiar with the bridge. "The drawbridge will be swinging back around in a few minutes."

Without a word, Becky dug into her cloth purse and pulled out the required number of coins.

They sat silently in the coach as a sailboat passed through the open drawbridge on its way down the river. Immediately after the sailboat-mast had cleared, the gears of the drawbridge screamed and groaned as it turned back into place. The coachman paid the toll and the horses lurched forward again, stepping carefully over the wooden planks of the bridge.

As they continued along the dirt path, talk with her mother had been impossible. Becky seemed to be lost in some other world.

After what seemed like an eternity, the horses slowed, grateful for the rest. With a sharp tug on the reins, the driver stopped them abruptly, shouting a loud "Whoa!"

When Lizzie looked out through the dust stirred up by the wagon, she saw they'd pulled up in front of an old, vine-covered inn. Before she could ask any questions, her mother pulled her out of the wagon and pushed her along the weedy path up to the front door.

Huge oaks and maples lined the path and darkened her way as she was hustled up to the entrance to the inn. What stories these old sentries could surely tell. How many visitors had come and gone this way in the past?

A young woman about her mother's age appeared behind the beveled panes of the heavy wooden door. She had to tug at the door a bit to open it because of its solid weight.

When it finally flew open, she called out, "Well, hallo to you, Becky. And I see you've brought your precious little Lizzie. What a lovely child she is." Lizzie immediately distrusted this lady. She didn't sound like she meant what she said.

Becky introduced the woman as Miss Rita Devlin, and the girl curtseyed. She held onto her mother's skirt with one hand for strength.

Miss Devlin and her mother exchanged a few words of conversation, which was mostly confusing to Lizzie. Then to her shock, Becky handed Miss Devlin her small brown carpet bag. In return, Miss Devlin handed her mother a plain envelope that was blank on the front.

Suddenly her mother bent low, so she could look into her child's eyes, which were wide with disbelief. "Now you be a good little girl until I come back for you," she instructed, absently brushing back a lock of her daughter's silky hair. "Mind Miss Devlin."

Lizzie shuddered as she looked into her mother's eyes and saw they were dark and distant. Before she could protest, her mother fled down the path to the wagon. All she could do was sob, "Mama."

"I'll be back soon, Lizzie, I promise," Becky shouted back as she turned to wave. The coachman quickly helped her into the vehicle, and then they were gone.

That was the last day the poor little girl ever saw her mother. She never returned as she'd promised.

Chapter Two

The Training

Miss Devlin was about the same age as her mother, in her early twenties, but they were as different as night and day. Her mother had long, curly raven hair, like Lizzie's, but her eyes were steel-gray and cool. She cast long, hard glances beneath the coal-black lashes, but she rarely gave voice to her inner feelings.

Lizzie wasn't sure what color Miss Devlin's hair was, because she used some sort of liquid from a brown bottle to change its color. Most of the time it was yellow and flaxen, the shade and texture of freshly cut straw.

Miss Devlin's black eyebrows and hooded brown eyes contrasted sharply with her straight blond hair. Her eyes could have been warm and comforting, but they weren't. She painted them with bright colors and drew black lines around the rims.

The villagers called her "brassy" behind her back and said she "put on airs," but Miss Devlin seemed to love the way she looked. She spent hours before the gilded mirror in her bedroom, brushing her lifeless hair. Sometimes Lizzie thought it would surely break off and fly away. After she was finished, Miss Devlin would stand back from the mirror, turning this way and that to admire herself from every angle.

"I look right nice today, don't ya think, Lizzie?" Miss Devlin would say, as she held her head in an awkward pose, neck twisted, chin pointed up.

"Yes, ma'am, you look very nice," Lizzie would lie, afraid of the consequences that might follow if she told the truth. There was so much about this woman to fear.

When her mother had first left her with Miss Devlin at the Light Horse Inn, as it was called, it hadn't been so bad. Even though she missed her mother and the tender caresses of Nana, Miss Devlin had cared for her needs. She'd also taught her to help around the large apartment where they lived above the alehouse.

Anyway, Lizzie was sure her mother would return soon and take her home. After all, she'd promised, hadn't she? Nana had always told her that if you make a promise, you had to keep it.

In the beginning it had been like a game at Miss Devlin's. Lizzie learned to sweep and scrub and polish, and Miss Devlin would reward her with small toys and snacks, like cookies or tarts. But soon the tasks became more difficult, the rewards disappeared and it wasn't any fun at all.

After several months Miss Devlin took her down to the alehouse and taught her to scrub the wooden floors with sand and salt and a big brush. She wouldn't let her stop until all traces of food stains and candle drippings were gone. Lizzie's fingers were soon red and swollen from the stinging salt, but she dared not complain.

Even though she said nothing, Miss Devlin saw Lizzie staring at her sore hands one day. "You're probably six years old by now," she snapped. "It's about time you pay your way."

"Yes ma'am," she replied rubbing her dry and swollen

fingers. Sometimes they would crack and bleed.

The next task was the laundry. Miss Devlin showed her how to carry bucket after bucket of water from the rain barrel to a big iron kettle in the back of the inn. Here they would heat the water that contained strong soap made from waste fats and lye. The lye was harsh on her skin too; it came from wood ashes through a separation process called leaching.

When the water was boiling hot, Lizzie was told to bring out all the tablecloths, towels, and cloth napkins from the inn. Then she had to stand on a big crate and stir the "brew" of linens with a long stick until everything was spotlessly clean. While they were still hot, she had to drag the linens out with the stick and put them in a large oak tub where she rinsed them in clean water. When Miss Delvin saw she was too small to ring them out, she reluctantly performed this task, but it was up to Lizzie to hang them on the clothesline to dry. By the time she'd hung up the last tablecloth, Lizzie was exhausted. She wanted to lie down for a nap, but Miss Devlin had many other chores in mind.

Day by day, Lizzie learned more: to pluck chickens, scale fish, hoe weeds, chop wood, clean out the big brick fireplace and on and on and on. By the time her training was completed, Lizzie had learned to perform every task that Miss Devlin hated.

Lizzie did enjoy one chore—baking the delicious bread and pies for the guests. It wasn't easy to knead the huge clumps of dough for the bread, but her effort was rewarded by the most enchanting aroma as the loaves baked in the big stone oven. And Lizzie knew that if she followed Miss Devlin's orders without arguing, she might be rewarded with a hot piece of pie and milk. How she did love that apple pie.

The weeks began to lengthen into months and the months into years. One day, after she'd been at the inn about two years, Miss Devlin got the old wooden cash drawer out and used it to teach Lizzie about money. She showed her what each coin was worth, how to count it and make change and how to store it in the proper slots of the drawer.

"You're bright enough, I'll say that for you," Miss Devlin said, somewhat surprised.

After she'd learned her lessons well, Miss Devlin was careful to explain to Lizzie, "This'll be your job now—to help me out here at the inn. 'Tisn't a hard job. We'll have fun, we will, and you'll learn a lot from me and from the gents who come in here."

Lizzie nodded silently, unable to argue. She had no one else to take care of her. With each passing month, it seemed more unlikely that her mother would return.

Once she asked Miss Devlin, "Where is my mother? When is she coming back?"

"She's not coming back," Miss Devlin replied as she counted the profits for the day. "She's gone."

What did that mean, she wondered? Had she left the area? Was she dead? Lizzie didn't know, but she did know one thing: she was alone.

It wasn't so much that Lizzie minded the hard work, but the worst part was that she had no friends and there was never time to play like the other children. Her days grew longer and longer. At night she would sink into her little bed in the bare room next to Miss Devlin's, too tired to sleep.

Was this to be her life forever? How could she bear it?

As she lay there, alone and tired, Lizzie would try unsuccessfully to remember her past. She had forgotten so much in those first days of fear. She couldn't remember the house or the lane on which it sat. The name Mystic Bridge, Nana, and Becky—that's all that was left.

All she could see now were disconnected images. Nana's soft gray hair, the twinkling blue eyes—eyes that looked so much like Lizzie's. But these images faded slowly, despite her efforts to keep them alive in her mind's eye. As time passed, she could barely remember if Nana had been tall or short, thin or round. Did she have a square chin, a small mouth?

The vague memories of Nana were all Lizzie had to hold onto, as she'd finally drift off to sleep. Nothing else in her hard life brought her much comfort or pleasure. She was sure her life would be so much better if she could just find Nana again.

The men who hung around the Light Horse Inn were a boisterous lot, mostly sailors and tradesmen and a few businessmen from the village. Sometimes they'd notice how hard Lizzie worked behind the big polished oak bar on a stool, and feel sorry for her. So they'd try to entertain her with little stories or jokes. Sometimes they even gave her small gifts—a stick of candy or a game they brought back from their travels.

Lizzie's favorite customer was a tall, slim sailor who always wore an old captain's hat. His name was Henry. He had a craggy face, molded by long years spent fighting storms and winds, but his hazel eyes were soft and sympathetic. He loved to tell her tales about his adventures on the sea and about the wild winds that blew his boat up and down the Atlantic seaboard.

Most of Henry's summers were spent there in Connecticut. The ocean breezes kept his little white cottage on Pine Island cool and inviting. Something about this area always pulled him back, he told Lizzie. But during the winter, he sailed the South Seas, trading anything of value he could acquire—some things that he wouldn't always talk about.

Lizzie yearned to know more about the world outside the Light Horse Inn. She'd listen to Henry's exciting tales as long as he would tell them. Once when she asked him quite innocently where the sun came from each day, he looked at her curiously.

"Why little matey, you should have learned about that in school by now. What grade are you in?"

She blinked and said softly, "I don't go to school. I have to help Miss Devlin here at the inn."

With that, the old sailor yelled, "Rita girl, come outta that kitchen!" In a moment Miss Devlin appeared, strutting with her hands on her swaying hips. She was definitely irritated by the interruption, as Henry shouted at her in mock rebuke.

"Why isn't this little tyke in school, Rita? You know she's old enough, she is. What is she now, maybe seven or eight?"

"I'm not rightly sure," Miss Devlin stared at the ceiling, trying to remember how old Lizzie was when she first got her. "Well, let's see, I think she was five when her Momma dropped her off, so she must be about nine by now. Never did know what day her birthday was. Her Momma left too quick—never had a chance to find out. 'Twas a shame, too.

"Yes, I know she should be agoin' to school with the other little scamps," she continued, "but I just can't spare her here. You know it's just me and her taking care of this big place. Don't rightly know what I'd be doin' without her."

With that, she gave Lizzie a big hug; the first one she could ever remember receiving from Miss Devlin.

Deciding there wasn't much more he could do to help
Lizzie, Henry nodded glumly. "Aye, guess your right, Rita,
but it don't seem fair to her. Bring me another spiced rum
then, you old hussy."

Henry turned to Lizzie and smiled sheepishly as he
shrugged his stooped shoulders. "Sorry I couldn't help you,
little one. Rita does work you too hard. You're too consarned
young. How much longer you going to be bound out to her?
Maybe you can go to school when you're done."

Lizzie barely heard his words, because she was still frozen
in place, shocked by the first sign of affection Miss Devlin
had ever shown her. The poor child didn't realize that Miss
Devlin's hug was just a game she was playing for Captain
Henry's benefit.

Finally she thought about the strange words he'd said.
"Bound out?" she repeated.

"That's where your mamma or papa signs a paper, and you
learn a job for two or three years. Then you're on your own.
Do you have papers?"

Henry didn't need an answer. He could tell from Lizzie's
blank stare that there was no official contract. "Lizzie," he
whispered behind his hand, "this sounds like servitude to me.
Rita may be keeping you here against the law."

The confusing conversation ended abruptly when Miss
Devlin's voice rang sharply from the back. "Lizzie, go fetch
the mop; I spilt some water behind the bar!"

Even though she often wondered about the strange events
that brought her here to Miss Devlin's, Lizzie never gave her
"guardian" much trouble, even when she was sad and tired.
But as winter turned to spring this year, she thought about
what Captain Henry had said. Why couldn't she go to school?

Why couldn't she learn more about the mysteries of the world that lay beyond the inn?

She longed to be able to read like the other children. What was in those books they always carried to and from school?

And so, when the brightly-dressed children of all ages streamed past the inn on the last day of school, she watched in dismay. Why must she spend every day, day after day, working in the inn?

Finally Lizzie summoned enough courage to ask. "Miss Devlin," she pleaded, "Could I please go to school next year?"

Miss Delvin didn't take much time to think about it. "No, Lizzie. Your place is here with me—in the inn. You know enough to help me. I never got no book learnin', and you won't be a-needin' it either."

Lizzie never said a word, but at that very moment, she made a decision that would change her life forever. Each night, in her cramped, little room, with no toys, no books, no pictures, she began planning her departure. She must leave Miss Devlin's now and find her way back to her real home— to Nana. It was time.

Once when she and Miss Devlin had taken a different path back from the market, they'd crossed another path with a big wooden sign that pointed to Mystic Bridge. Although she couldn't read, Lizzie knew a few words, and she recognized these two. She knew when she saw the sign that she'd been this way before. It had triggered a vague recollection of the coach with the big horses that had brought her mother and her this way a few years ago.

Was Nana still in Mystic Bridge? She might have moved away long ago. But if Lizzie could find her, she knew Nana would make sure she went to school. She would go to Mystic

Bridge. If she couldn't find Nana, she would have to find a life of her own. There was no other way.

Now as the rain beat down, Lizzie, dressed in the disguise of a boy, ran along the path to Mystic Bridge. She was miserably wet and apprehensive, but she was free from the demanding Miss Devlin, and free from the lonely life at the inn. She was on her way home!

When she had planned her departure from the Light Horse Inn, Lizzie carefully considered when she'd leave and what she'd need most to live on her own for a while. She knew that if she couldn't find Nana right away, she would need to prepare herself well to survive, out of sight, so no one would find her while she looked.

Although Lizzie had no schooling, she was a sharp observer of human nature during her days at the inn. She realized that men and boys of the community had a great deal more freedom of movement than their female counterparts. The women and girls were sheltered and protected by the men or their parents and were rarely seen alone. Until she could find Nana, Lizzie needed freedom to be alone and move about.

It would be hard to make it alone as a girl even though she knew she could do it; she was sure someone would try to stop her. Girls were viewed as weak and less intelligent, and they were never given the opportunity for jobs—even poor ones.

Yes, the answer was simple, yet complicated to achieve. She would become a boy!

CHAPTER 3
The Plan

Once she'd made the decision to leave as a boy, Tagger began to make or collect the things she would need to assume the disguise and to survive until she could find Nana. For days, she studied the men who came to the inn until she could mimic their posture and gestures.

She knew what she would need to take, and one by one she began to collect the items from the trash at the inn or in backyard dump sites in town. She'd begun her collection of "essentials" one day, when she was working in the kitchen at the inn. Miss Devlin was serving a dignified gentleman his noonday dinner at one of the little wooden tables in front of the bar. The gentleman was well-to-do and always left substantial tips, so Miss Devlin was going out of her way to meet all of his needs.

"A little more of our fine coffee, sir?" Miss Devlin had crooned. "How about some of our fresh-baked tarts for the gentleman?"

"No, no, I'm fine, Rita," he'd answered, waving her off with a laugh. "Just go wait on your other customers, so I can read these papers, before it's time to go back to work."

Seeing that Miss Devlin was fully occupied, Lizzie ran to the large trash box in the corner of the kitchen and looked for the old paring knife she's seen Miss Devlin throw away that morning.

Shifting her gaze to the front of the bar, Lizzie made sure Miss Devlin wasn't watching, and then she quickly stuck the knife into her high-topped boot. The knife had a broken tip, but it was sharp and would serve many purposes.

Over the next few weeks, she hid several other items in her apron and the pockets of her dress. Soon she had a dented spoon, a bent fork, a chipped plate, and a cup without a handle—all tucked safely in the bottom of her carpet bag that she kept under her bed. A real find was a box of matches a customer had dropped just outside the entrance to the inn—still dry!

Her biggest "treasures" came from the large wooden crate where Miss Devlin threw the items left by the guests who'd stayed at the inn. She had an opportunity to dig through it one day when Miss Devlin went to town.

First she found an old white shirt with a yoke and three buttons at the neck. It was ripped in the back and had a streak of grease on the side. Either the guest had left it by mistake or perhaps on purpose. In either case, Lizzie was thrilled. She could easily fix the rip and scrub the grease out of the side. It was too big, of course, but it would be covered by the black cloak that she'd worn the day she was brought to the inn.

And britches! She'd about given up, when she dug to the very bottom of the crate and found them. She couldn't believe that someone had left them by accident. They were old, but quite serviceable, and were made of sturdy cotton material They came way down over her knees, but by using a leather belt she also found, she could hitch them up until they looked presentable.

One day when the wind had whipped up from the ocean and blown through Groton, a boy had lost his wide-brimmed felt hat. Although he and his father had searched a long time for it, it had landed in a thicket, and they had failed to see it. They finally gave up. A few days later, Lizzie passed the same spot, and being shorter and more observant, had found it. Now her boy's outfit was complete.

This was an admirable start, but Lizzie knew it wasn't enough. Whenever Miss Devlin sent her on errands, she'd rummage through the backyard dump sites like a scavenger.

This effort paid off when she was fortunate enough to find the metal head of a hatchet. In her customary manner, she roamed around town, tagging along with the local craftsmen and shop owners, asking how it could be fixed. The village smithy finally took pity on her and fashioned a handle that fit snugly into the opening of the head. Her very own hatchet! The smithy looked at her with surprise. He'd never seen a child so excited over a tool. "Now you be careful, Lizzie," he warned. "I ground that head, and it's mighty sharp."

"Oh I will, and now it's all mine. Thank you so much. Please don't tell Miss Devlin, though," she pleaded. "She wouldn't understand."

"I promise," he winked.

It was a little harder to hide the hatchet from Miss Devlin. Lizzie carried it home in the pocket of her cloak, but then what? Where would she hide it at the inn? Ah, she had an idea! She'd hide it in the back of the big fireplace in the kitchen. Since she was always the one to clean it out, she knew Miss Devlin would never find the hatchet there.

As luck would have it, Miss Devlin bought some new towels and washcloths one day in late spring. No one ever threw away old toweling in those days, but fortunately for Lizzie, Miss Devlin retired them to the pantry to be used as rags. Lizzie wasn't greedy; she took only two ragged towels and two washcloths. Surely Miss Devlin wouldn't miss them or the partially used bar of soap she took.

When Lizzie had come to live with Miss Devlin, her mother had packed a tiny sewing kit in her satchel. Nana had taught her that females should always be prepared to mend and darn; she thought that Nana had probably given her the kit initially. The thread had been used up long ago, but there were still two needles and a thimble. It was a simple matter for Lizzie to collect bits of thread and wrap them around little wooden sticks, when Miss Devlin had her do the mending. Soon she had quite a collection of colors: red, light blue, white, black and yellow.

The hardest item to find was a spade, and it was essential. If she couldn't find Nana right away, she knew she'd have to plant a garden and harvest some vegetables in the summer. She'd carefully stowed away extra seeds, onion sets and potato eyes from the garden at the inn and was now prepared to plant peas, lettuce, green beans, carrots, potatoes, onions and squash when she had her own garden. But where would she find a spade?

Lizzie followed the farmers around for a week when they came to town, but no one ever had an old spade, at least not one they were willing to give up. The days were ticking by, and Lizzie knew she would have to leave soon or she wouldn't have time to get her garden started. She finally decided she would just have to use a broken chard from a cracked clay pot she'd found to till her garden. But then one day the problem was solved.

Whenever Lizzie went to the mercantile store for Miss Devlin, she went the long way around and checked the backyard dump sites. There was nothing on this particular day. She'd picked it bare of anything valuable, but as she was walking back to the inn, she passed the small brook that fed into the Mystic River.

She always enjoyed coming this way. The sun lit up the flowing water in the brook as it ran over rocks and shale cliffs on its way to the river. It cheered her to watch it, but today was even better.

Sticking out from under a log near the brook was a small spade! It was a little rusted and bent, but it was all in one piece and would serve her quite well. She had everything she needed! It was time to leave!

The night before her departure, Tagger had made one final decision that she dreaded. If she were to truly pose as a boy, she must cut her long, dark curls. At first she thought that she could hide her hair under her hat, but then she began to notice that men were required to doff their hats to passersby on the street and remove them when they were inside. There was no choice.

Just before she went to bed, she used Miss Devlin's scissors to whack off her beautiful curls. She planned to leave the next morning before she could be seen. Lately, Miss Devlin had taken to being a slug-a-bed in the mornings, too tired to rouse herself after her late nights with the customers. But what would she do with the hair? If Miss Devlin found it, she would know Lizzie had changed her appearance. So she quickly gathered the curly locks and tucked them into a bag to be thrown in a trash dump several houses away as she passed by.

Just when she thought she had worked out all the details, it hit her. What was she preparing to do here? Leave the only place where she'd had shelter for the past four years? Start out on a lonely road to find someone who might not even exist anymore?

And what if she didn't find Nana? Children without parents were typically placed in homes, girls to be taught useful skills and cared for, boys to be apprenticed. She knew that. People believed that children should not live alone.

And yet, that was exactly what she had to do. If she couldn't find Nana, she wouldn't live with anyone else. She had had four bad years of depending upon someone else, and as young as she was, she would not do it again. She had become strong and grownup and satisfied with herself.

Being alone was not always bad. Still, it was going to be hard to survive—very hard.

CHAPTER 4
The Cottage

Tagger wrapped her right arm tightly around her chest and gripped her left arm as she ran, trying to shield herself from the wind and the pinging raindrops. She clutched her little brown carpet bag with her many "essentials" tightly in her left hand.

Her cloak twisted itself around her. The big pockets that lined the inside of it were filled with her remaining possessions, the hatchet wrapped in a towel, the spade, the cup, and the plate. The bulky contents banged against her legs as she tried to run, and caused her to stumble crazily along the muddy path.

She began to tire. What could she do? She wanted to cry, but she knew it would do no good. No one would hear her, and it would only tire her more.

Suddenly she saw a smaller path that branched off to the right. At the end of it was a wooden structure, huddled in the gloom. It looked like a small cottage, and it appeared to be abandoned.

Maybe she could at least dry off and wait out the storm. There was no choice; she was desperate. She quickly ran the distance to the old building, careful not to stumble in the muddy ruts along the way.

Just to make sure it was deserted, Tagger knocked timidly on the white, paint-chipped door. The hinges were rusted, but she could see the door was unlocked.

She waited and then pounded louder. After several seconds she tried the handle. She couldn't open it on the first attempt, but when she pushed very hard, using all her weight, the door gave way. She burst into the room. The wind whipped in behind her, nearly knocking her off her feet. She had to use all her strength to re-close the warped door.

Exhausted from running and pushing on the door, Tagger sank to the dusty floor, grateful to have a dry place to rest. She lay panting for several minutes, trying to catch her breath.

After a while she sat up and looked around the cottage. To her surprise it was in fairly good condition. Yes, peeling paint hung from the walls like parchment rolls and cobwebs were thick on the ceiling, but she could see many other good features.

There was a white, stone fireplace, crumbling on one side, but still serviceable. Three long, bare wooden shelves hung on the wall, and there was an intriguing storage box in the corner. Several of the windows had jagged cracks, but they were all in place and would keep the rain out.

She pulled herself up, still slightly out of breath, and went to the storage box. It was white too, with the same rusted hinges as the front door. The rusted tongue of the latch hung over the lock loop. Evidently the previous owner had taken the lock—that is, if there had ever been one. The top came open easily when she pulled up on the tongue.

At first, she thought the box was empty, but upon closer examination, she saw there was something in the bottom. It was black and made of some type of fabric. She brought it out, unfolded it and in the lingering light, saw that it was a woolen blanket. It was old and worn around the facing, but luckily the moths had never found it, and it was clean and dry. What an important discovery this was!

She took off her wet clothes, hung them over the box and wrapped the blanket around her. Cuddled in the corner, happy to be dry, she was already starting to feel better.

Soon she was asleep, dreaming of better times. The few images from her earlier life before the inn swam before her eyes, disconnected, disjointed. But at least she was free from the oppressive life at the inn.

This was the first night of Tagger's new life. When she awoke early the next morning the skies had cleared. She decided she would stay here on her own on the outskirts of Portersville, just north of Noank, at least for now, until she found Nana.

She had no choice, really. The deserted cottage was on the west side of the river from the village of Mystic Bridge, and she remembered the drawbridge that had to be crossed. And she remembered the coins it took. She would need money before she could cross the bridge to her hometown.

CHAPTER 5
The Secret

Tagger wasn't worried that Miss Devlin would follow her and doubted she would even contact the authorities to try to find her. Even though Tagger was confused by Captain Henry's conversation about servitude, she was certain that Miss Devlin had done something wrong and would not want to be involved with the law.

And besides, if Miss Devlin did try to find her, she would be looking for the girl, Lizzie, not the boy, Tagger.

Beneath her ragged look and jagged haircut, Tagger was really a lovely child. When it wasn't cut short, her long, dark hair had hung in lustrous, natural waves, but it was her eyes that were so magnificent. They were the color of a cloudless blue sky and almost too large for her delicately shaped face.

Her face was nearly heart-shaped, but the smooth curves of her cheeks ended in a strong jaw line and a determined chin. There was something about her that seemed from another time, almost as though she were dreaming and seeing into the future. Her eyes said so much.

She knew her face would be a disadvantage to her disguise, so she would have to keep her head low when she encountered other people. But her undeveloped girlish body was an advantage. She was sure that "Tagger" would go undetected, at least for awhile.

Even though life with Miss Devlin had been hard and demanding, she knew how to run a house. Tagger had learned many important duties from her. Some of this training would help her survive until she could get the money to cross the bridge and find Nana and her old home. She would live here in the cottage; it would do for a while. Nobody would come here, because it was off the beaten path, and for some reason, deserted. She was determined to find enough to eat and to make it on her own.

She knew how to gather wood and build a fire. She could cook whatever food she found or grew, and she knew how to wash her few eating utensils and clothes in the cold little stream that ran behind the cottage.

Now that she was on her own, she told herself, she would have to work quickly to get her garden planted and her crops harvested before fall.

Tagger was full of enthusiasm that first morning and anxious to start her garden. As she bathed in the cool stream, she wondered who owned this cottage. Judging by the thickness of the dust on the shelves, it seemed to have been idle for months or even years. Surely no one would mind if she stayed here awhile.

When she was dry and dressed, she took her little spade out to a patch of earth behind the cottage and began turning the dirt in preparation for planting. The ground was wet from the soaking rain the day before, but it was still slow going, because the spade was so small. Tagger was happy to see that the soil was rich and brown though; she knew her vegetables would grow quickly.

The sun beat down heavily as she planted the seeds and sets she'd brought from Miss Devlin's. She set the lettuce seeds in a mounded section she'd formed, spacing them far apart, so the heads would have plenty of room to grow. Next she planted neat, alternating rows of peas and green beans, and then she made another mound where she planted green onion sets. She had brought potato eyes and squash and carrot seeds as well, which she planted next to the onions.

Exhausted, she stood up finally to survey her garden. She wiped the dirt from her face and arms with one of the old washcloths from the inn. Yes, she was satisfied with her work. Now all she had to do was pull weeds and water the soil, and she would have vegetables. But she knew it would be quite a while; she would have to have some fresh food in the meantime.

What would she eat? She'd brought some day-old bread from Miss Devlin's which was stale now, and she'd salvaged two baked potatoes that hadn't been eaten by the patrons of the tavern the night before she left. She'd get by today and maybe tomorrow, but what about the next day and the one after that?

Tagger began to prowl the woods like an animal looking for wild fruit, mushrooms and edible roots. She found some wild strawberries in a sunny patch near the path and ate them immediately. And then she found a few green cherries that were just beginning to ripen, but all she could do with these was pick them, and store them in the wooden box in the cottage to ripen.

After two days of cleaning the tiny cottage, she grew very hungry, even weak. What was she going to do? She couldn't go back to Miss Devlin's, and yet she knew that if she didn't eat pretty soon, she would lose her strength.

And how would she find Nana? She had no way to earn money to cross the bridge to Mystic Bridge. She knew she'd made the right decision to leave Miss Devlin's, but doubts began to nag at her as the hunger increased.

CHAPTER 6
The Hook

Tagger had been on her own for almost three days when she awoke to a gray mist hanging over the woods. She shook herself awake. Her bed was made of leaves and rags she'd found, and her black blanket covered them. It was actually fairly comfortable, and she would have liked to sleep a bit more, but the gnawing hunger in the pit of her belly propelled her to action.

She knew she had to find some real food today. She'd have to find work of some kind. When she'd been out exploring the area surrounding the cottage, she realized she'd stumbled upon a fairly secluded area in between two villages, Noank to the south and Portersville to the north. Portersville appeared to be the more populated of the two villages and the one most likely to need the services of a young boy.

So far no one had observed her living here. She'd purposely stayed out of sight, but now she would have to go out among people and take her chances.

After she'd washed in the stream, she dressed in the masculine outfit. Satisfied that she looked as much like a boy as possible, she set off in the direction of Portersville. Just before she reached the village, she saw the brick lodging house she'd spotted earlier when she was searching for food.

Since it was set on the outskirts of town, nestled in a grove of pine trees, the lodging house did a good business. It was quiet here and the guests could rest peacefully. Tagger's plan was to work in exchange for some bread.

Bread was a staple food during this period in New England, and everyone relied on it for its nutrient value. Tagger's lack of bread was a major concern to her and a need she had to fill.

As she neared the back of the lodging house, she wondered what she would find there. Rejection, rudeness? Timidity took over, and she had to have a talk with herself to regain her courage. Resolutely, she climbed the back steps and tapped on the heavy door.

After what seemed like an eternity, the door opened wide and revealed an older woman dressed in a long, tan-colored dress covered by a huge apron that reached nearly to the floor. When Tagger looked down at the long apron, she noticed something that gave her an idea.

"Well, what is it you'd be wanting here, boy?" the lady boomed. At first Tagger was unnerved, but then she saw the woman break into a big smile and liked her immediately.

"Good morning, ma'am, my name's Tagger," she said with her head bowed as much as possible to hide her feminine face beneath the hat. "I need to find some work."

"Well, we're always looking for help. What can you do?" the woman responded in a businesslike manner.

"I noticed your floor needs cleaning," Tagger replied, pointing behind the woman to the filthy kitchen floor covered with fat drippings and soot from the fireplace. "I can make that floor look like new, and all I'd like is some bread in return."

The woman frowned, appraising Tagger from head to foot.

Finally, she smiled again and said, "You've got yourself a job, young fellow. My name's Betty. I'm the head cook here. Can you do it right now, before we serve the dinner guests? You're right about that floor. Nasty, it is."

Tagger breathed a sigh of relief. The disguise had worked, at least so far. She agreed to start immediately, and the deal was finalized. She removed her hat as she entered the lodge. No reaction! Good!

Even though she was hungry and weak, Tagger cleaned with a vengeance. She used sand and salt and a brush to scrub the kitchen floor just the way Miss Devlin had taught her. She didn't stop until the floor was spotless. Betty agreed that Tagger had made the floor look like new and paid her with a loaf of coarse bread and some meat chunks.

There was a small oak table with four chairs by the fireplace where some of the workers ate, and Betty asked Tagger if she would like to eat her food there. Tagger was so hungry that she readily agreed, and she said little as she gobbled her meat and half a loaf of bread. This was the most food she'd eaten since she'd left Miss Devlin's.

"My, you are hungry," Betty observed. "When was the last time you ate?"

Tagger stopped eating long enough to answer. "Oh, this morning," she lied. "I just have a big appetite." She couldn't let Betty know she was starving, or Betty would tell someone from town and there would be trouble.

Betty thought this over for a minute. "Yes, and I suppose all that scrubbing helped your appetite. You're new in these parts, aren't you?"

Oh no, the questions! Tagger had rehearsed in her mind what she would say if anyone raised questions. "Yes, we just came here from Groton," she replied assuming her best imitation of a boy's voice.

"Where you staying?" Betty continued.

"In the cottage in the woods just south of here," Tagger replied nonchalantly.

But Betty was persistent. "Your parents and you?"

"No, just Pa and I. We came down from Groton," she began. It was the story she would use with the rest of the adults she encountered. "He sailed on a ship that went to the south seas, and when they got back, he got sick. The doctor said it was ague, the fever disease, and it comes and goes. He has to rest for a while until he's well enough to find a job. He thought maybe he'd find a job at a shipyard when he's better." Tagger had listened well to Captain Henry's tales of the sea, which helped her make this story sound true.

"That's too bad, ague is a powerful bad disease," Betty sympathized. "People traipsin' off to strange parts of the world like that, catching diseases! Still, we've got it here too. Well there's plenty of jobs to find in these parts," Betty assured her. "Shipbuilding is really picking up here; they say this is a good place to build ships because of all the right trees, white pine, white oak, white ash. Also there are many deep spots in the river, where they can build the tall ships."

Tagger took this in without speaking, reluctant to offer any more information than necessary.

"Say, isn't that cottage you're talking about the one that was abandoned after that Owen fellow died?" Betty asked.

"Don't know," Tagger replied. "We just got here, and we're just using it until Pa is well, and we can build our own place."

"Then you probably haven't heard yet," Betty said. "They say that cottage is haunted."

Tagger asked simply, "Why?"

"Well," Betty began, "there was a young man in that cottage, just starting out, he was. I think his name was Richard Owen. He started a gristmill here and was making really fine corn meal. Owen was clever and was always looking for ways to improve the meal and figure ways to sell it cheaper. He was using the waterpower to grind other things too—flaxseed oil and white flour.

"One day, he went to a fishing pier down at Noank, when a storm was coming up from the south. They say he went there a lot; he'd just sit by the water and dream of new inventions. The storm came up real quick and caught him off guard. When he tried to run, a gale caught him. Guess he stumbled and fell off the side of the pier. He couldn't swim and no one was around. Drowned right there in the sound. They found his body after the storm was over, floating face down near the pier.

"No one ever goes to the pier or his house," she continued. "They think they're haunted—a fellow thought he saw Owen's ghost on the pier one night."

Tagger didn't care much about superstitions. She was actually happy to hear that people thought the cottage was haunted. Maybe this would assure her some time alone until she could get her garden started and find some way to get money.

When Tagger had finished her dinner and helped wash the dishes, she asked Betty if she could come back later and help out again. Betty was only too happy to agree.

"As hard as you work, you can come back anytime you want," she said. When she saw Tagger gather up the other half loaf of bread, she assumed she was taking it to her pa. "Here," she said, moving to the stove, "Take some of this broth for your pa too."

Tagger nodded eagerly, "Yes, he'd like that."

Betty filled a pottery crock with the warm, golden chicken broth, and Tagger took it happily. "Thank you, ma'am. I'll be back to help out again. Good bye."

This was a good day. She had some food and a source for getting more. She was a step closer to having a true home.

A couple of days later, when all the bread and broth were gone, Tagger returned to the lodging house. The kitchen was still in decent shape, but Betty had some dishes for her to wash in return for half a loaf of bread. The bread helped nourish her, but it wasn't enough; she needed fruit and meat.

So after she left the lodge she was out in the woods again searching for something to eat. She came to another big cherry tree and saw that there were small cherries just beginning to pop out in red towards the top.

The tree forked at the center, forming a saddle-like seat. It was a perfect place for a child to climb up. With one big jump, she was up in the fork, grabbing skinny branches to pull herself higher. She found several clusters of new cherries halfway to the top and hoped these were ripe. She picked one and tasted it. Blewee! It was too sour to eat too. Ever resourceful, she picked all the cherries she could reach and stuffed them into the pockets of her cloak. They'd be ripe in a couple of days, but that didn't solve her immediate problem.

She shimmied down the tree trunk and began searching through the thicket near the path for anything edible. After a while, she spotted a cluster of ripe, purple raspberries and reached out to pluck them. They were delicious, her favorite. She'd have to remember this spot.

As she savored the tart, black pulp, she spotted an especially big cluster of ripe berries low on the bush, beneath a thick mass of crinkled leaves. She'd almost missed them at first.

When she reached up under the leafy branch, something pricked her finger, and she jerked her hand away. Bending down for a closer look, she saw a fish hook with a length of line tied to it. It was wrapped around the branches of the bush.

"One of the fisherman from the village must have lost this," she said to herself. "What a lucky discovery."

Tagger frequently saw fishermen dragging their lines to the harbor in Groton. She liked to follow them and watch them at their work, when Miss Devlin would allow her. Normally they took hand lines out in their boats for large catches, but sometimes they set lines or used pound nets around the banks of the harbor.

It was important to Tagger to carefully unwind the hook and line from the bush without harming the raspberries. She didn't want to lose even one.

The hook was fairly large, with an angled barb at the point. It was attached to a length of cotton cord, maybe twenty-five feet long, and was tied about eighteen inches up from the end. At the end of the cord was a heavy gray, lead weight, like a little anchor. After she'd sized up her find, she immediately wound the cord up in a lose ball around the weight and tucked the hook inside.

Then she stuffed the rest of the berries into her mouth and chewed slowly, trying to make the taste last as long as possible. Finally she swallowed; time to move on. Unfortunately she was still hungry.

Her step was lighter as she sauntered along the path back to the cottage though. The smell of summer filled her nostrils as she breathed in the aroma of sassafras leaves and honeysuckle. She didn't have much to eat, but she had a new tool—a fishing pole of sorts. Maybe this would be the start of a new adventure.

When she reached the cottage, she searched about for something to use for bait. Her belongings were sparse, and she couldn't see anything that would look appealing to a fish.

And then it came to her. Worms! That was it; she needed worms. She'd wait for nightfall and try to catch some in the moist leaves near the stream. She didn't know much about the slimy critters, but she'd seen them venture out of their holes at night to stretch themselves. How hard could it be to just pick them up and put them in the cracked clay pot she'd brought?

Later that evening, when a lone owl was scanning the ground for his dinner, Tagger was out hunting too. But she was after fat, wriggling night crawlers.

When she crept out on the path to the stream, she saw them everywhere. Their pinkish skin glimmered in the dim light of her candle. But when she lunged to grab them with her fingers, they were quicker, much quicker. They weren't easy to catch, at all. They had an uncanny ability to wriggle back to their damp holes quicker than she could stop them.

She began to realize that even though the worms would stretch themselves all the way out, they kept the tips of their tails anchored in their holes. This way, the slightest movement around them would cause them to pull themselves back into the refuge of their homes. Very clever!

Her catch was disappointing. She estimated she would

need at least half a dozen night crawlers, but she only managed to catch one plump crawler and a small red worm. They'd have to do; it was getting late. The moon was already high in the sky, and Tagger wanted a good night's sleep before her adventure tomorrow.

CHAPTER 7
The Fish

A fleeting ray of sunlight pierced the heavy, gray clouds and woke Tagger from a deep sleep. At first she wanted to linger in her makeshift bed, but when she remembered her plans for the day, she jumped to her feet.

Without a moment's hesitation, she washed herself in the stream. When she was satisfied she was clean and fresh, she pulled on the boy's clothes. She had washed everything the evening before in the stream, sparingly using the soap she'd brought from the inn, soap she'd used to scrub the floors and windows. Since she had no clothesline, she'd hung the clothes on a branch to dry.

Tagger had brought one dress with her and wore it while she did her washing. She realized it was risky if someone saw her dressed like this, but so far, no one had passed by this part of the woods. She needed more clothes suitable for a boy.

She shrugged into the black cloak and tied it around her neck. In the back of her mind, she wondered what she would do about a winter coat. By then she would have surely found Nana—if she was there. But there was no time to worry about it now; she had more important matters to attend to.

A quick check of the pocket of her cloak confirmed that

the fishing hook and line were still there. Good! And the line was neatly wound around the weight, just as she'd left it. She'd polished the hook carefully the night before, and now it felt fine and smooth to her touch.

Next she walked purposefully over to a shelflike rock at the edge of the stream. She'd found a wooden box with slats and had set it partially in the water. When the stream water flowed through it, it created a cool spot where she could store food to keep it from spoiling, that is if she ever had any to store.

Now she reached in and removed the cracked clay pot that was covered loosely with a leaf. A bit of dirt and moss was stuffed inside. She lifted the leaf and peered in at the two worms she'd caught the night before. They were still quite lively.

All right, she was ready. Without any more delay, she bounded off through the thick carpet of leaves and pine needles surrounding the cottage. This time she headed south, toward the tiny village of Noank. During her wanderings, she'd learned that Noank extended out toward a large body of water, which she guessed to be a sound. Based on the conversations she'd heard at the inn, she thought that a sound would be the best place to catch fish.

She'd walked about forty-five minutes across the narrow paths cut through the woods until she caught the unmistakable fragrance of the sea. Suddenly it appeared! The grandeur of the ocean. She'd seen it many times during her short lifetime, but it thrilled her more each time. The indescribable blue, green, gray color of the water which changed each time the weather changed.

The first time she'd seen the ocean, she was frightened.

The sight and sound of the surf intimidated her, but Nana had been there with her. It was one of her few memories. One of the things that nothing could drive out of her mind was the endless, rhythmic, sound of the waves as they marched to the shore, fired their explosive report and then retreated back into the sea to gather more strength for the next attack.

Nana had held her hand and told her it was safe. When Tagger had grown more accustomed to the sight and sound of the surf, they had taken off their shoes and stockings and run joyously through the waves.

Now that she was older, her fear of the ocean was gone, but she had so many unanswered questions. Where did the waves come from and what kept the sea from spilling out of its boundaries? Why were the waves close to shore sometimes and farther away at others?

Once when Tagger had gone to town for Miss Devlin, she'd heard the silliest conversation at the livery stable. The smithy in the blacksmith shop was re-shoeing a black mare for a tall, well-dressed businessman.

The man appeared to be intelligent and well educated, but he had actually said something about the earth being round. She was sure the man was crazy and wondered why the smithy didn't laugh right in his face. Why, even she knew that if the earth were round, the water from the sea would surely drain off and dump right out into the sky.

Today, she saw that the sound was still flat, as it should be, all the way to where it met the sky. But it was different here in the sound than it had been at the beach with Nana. The waves were calmer here and the shoreline had rocks and cliffs instead of the smooth sandy beach where Nana had taken her. The salty taste of the air and the wind tousling her hair heightened her excitement. She was going to catch some fish but wondered where she should go to catch them.

It was important to have just the right spot, away from the other fishermen but also where the fish were biting. And then she remembered what Betty had said about the haunted pier where Richard Owen had met his death. It didn't take her long to find it. It was the only pier with no one on it, and it showed obvious signs of disrepair. Fortunately it was on the far north side of the village too, far removed from where the other piers were clustered.

Tagger didn't have time for silly superstitions, so she strode out onto the pier with confidence. She was just happy to have found such a perfect spot for fishing. The pier was low to the water and about one hundred yards long. The gray, weathered planks sagged in spots and many of the boards were missing. But just as she skillfully skirted a gaping hole, the sun burst forth. Yes, this would be a good place.

The waves splashed on the shore rhythmically, bringing the foamy salt mounds to rest along the rocky shoreline. The scene before her momentarily awed Tagger, as she walked to the end of the pier.

Although she had work to do, she sat quietly for just a few moments with her legs dangling over the rough wooden edge of the pier. She wondered what lay across the sea. Was there more land out there with people on it, or was it just an endless rolling of waves?

Her old friend Henry the sailor had told her once that there was a place called England out there somewhere, far away. And she'd heard too that people from there had come to this area long ago. That was hard for her to believe. No one, she thought, would ever have the courage to sail out into that endless stretch of blue-green water, not knowing if they'd ever find land.

She shook herself out of her reverie and pulled the hook and the line from her pocket. The hook glistened in the sun.

When she took the red worm from the clay pot, she paused. It was difficult to thread it onto the hook, because she so loved all of the living creatures. But Tagger knew the scheme of nature was such that sometimes human beings had to kill animals and fish to keep themselves alive.

She flinched slightly as the hook pierced the squirming worm. Just for a moment, she had to close her eyes, but somehow she managed to arrange the worm on the metal shaft so it would make a tempting meal for a fish.

Finally satisfied with her bait, she threw the line out as far as she could. It floated for a moment on the rolling waves and then sank quickly as the sinker pulled it down. Because the hook was set a foot and a half up from the weight, the bait was drifting just above the sandy bottom where the fish normally fed. This was the way the other fisherman seemed to do it; she hoped she had it right.

She tied the other end of the line to a block of wood she'd brought from the woodpile behind the cottage and held it firmly in her hand. Now all she had to do was wait.

"I wonder how long it will take," she thought. Several minutes, maybe half an hour, passed as she sat in the sunlight watching the water and thinking of what lay beyond.

All was calm, except for the ever-present murmur of the ocean. And then it happened! The line jerked. The block of wood cut into her fingers.

For a moment she was so surprised she couldn't move. And then, too late, she pulled the wood to try to set the hook.

Whatever had struck at her bait was gone now. Only the bare hook dangled from the double knot when she pulled in the line. She stared at it sadly. How could she have been so careless?

The black cloak was too hot on the sunny pier, so she removed it. Hunger pains began to gnaw at her, and she knew that she would have to eat something soon to keep up her strength.

Only the night crawler was left. If she weren't careful, she'd lose it too, to a fish much cagier than herself. A little more determined this time, she baited the hook quickly and threw the line out again. This time, she got it out a little farther.

She was much more alert and prepared now as she sat perched forward, waiting. This was a new skill she'd have to master. She believed it was called patience.

A long time passed, and she grew tired in the uncomfortable position. How long would it take?

She held the "fishing pole" in her left hand and slowly dug into the pocket of her cloak with her right hand to find her last remaining crust of bread she'd brought. She munched quietly and began to feel more resolute about waiting for her first fish.

The sun was beating straight down now; telling her that it must be midday. She'd become uncomfortable in the tensed position, but she only dared shift her weight occasionally and in a way that wouldn't disturb the line.

It was more than hunger that kept her here. It was also the need to prove to herself that she could accomplish this. If she could meet this challenge, it would make her stronger for other ones in the future.

Oh! Another bite! The line tugged and cut through the

water. She reacted immediately and jerked the line just hard enough to set the hook but not too hard to jerk it out of the fish's mouth.

She pulled on the line firmly, but slowly. Yes, it was still there and it was pulling back—hard! Her excitement grew as she jumped to her feet. She quickly eased the line up and wrapped it around the block, over and over.

The fish was coming up to the surface. She could see it now. It was large, with blue-green scales, and it flailed about wildly, stirring the water around it.

It became more difficult to continue to wind the line, because she couldn't do it fast enough to keep it taut. So she dropped the block of wood and pulled the line, hand over hand, with a steady motion. The excess line fell on the pier.

Could she outlast the fish? She was shaking— using every bit of her strength. Her small arms were barely a match for the powerful fish. Finally she hauled it over the edge of the pier, but not before it jumped out of the water, shaking its head, in one final attempt to dislodge the hook from its mouth.

She watched admiringly as the lovely fish danced back and forth across the wood planks, flopping with loud "thunks," and then bending itself double. It scared her when it snapped its toothy mouth in her direction, apparently trying to bite at her. She mustn't get too close. She didn't realize that fish had such big teeth, but this kind certainly did—strong, pointed ones.

As she watched with awe she knew she'd succeeded! This was the first victory in her young life, and it gave her an inner strength she'd never known before.

After a while the fish slowed its frantic slapping about and lay quietly; the only movement was the desperate fanning of its gills and the snapping of its jaws. Occasionally, it would muster a last bit of strength and try unsuccessfully to fling itself back into the water. Tagger hated the sight of this courageous creature fighting for life, so she removed her boot and mercifully struck the back of its head. It quivered once and then lay completely still.

It was a beautiful fish, shiny, with bluish green scales on its back, blending to almost white scales on its belly. She wasn't sure what kind it was, but she knew it must be a game fish because of its wonderful fight. She'd heard many names for fish like striped bass, bluefish, mackerel and flounder, but she had no idea which name fit this one.

For the first time, she realized she had no way to carry the fish back to her cottage. Looking around, she saw something up the shore about fifty yards away, tangled in sea grass.

She ran quickly to the spot where the pier met the shore and jumped off onto the small rocks and sand. Stumbling crazily, she reached a pile of trash blowing in the light breeze. In it was a piece of white muslin cloth. Although it was dusty and wrinkled, it was fairly clean.

She dipped the cloth in the water and wrung it out several times. Finally she dipped it one last time and brought it out dripping with salt water. Without wringing it, she held it out from her and ran back up the pier. She wrapped the lifeless fish in the sopping cloth and hefted it up in her arms.

The fish was heavy; she guessed it weighed three or four pounds. Would she be able to carry it all the way back to the cottage like this? It seemed to grow heavier as she walked. But it was a labor of love, because this fish meant success and a good meal to come.

A breeze picked up as she walked. It felt good and gave her a little spurt of energy. But by the time she reached the cottage, she was beginning to tire.

Right now the familiar hunger pains were all she could think about. She'd rest later. She quickly began gathering chunks of wood twigs and small sticks and placed them in a spiral pattern within the round circle of stones that formed the boundary of the outdoor fireplace the previous owner had made. Then she stuffed some leaves and dry milkweed pods and fibers between the sticks and lit them with one of her wooden matches.

As the fire popped and crackled, she cleaned the fish. It was a struggle, because her only tool was the old unpointed knife she'd brought from the inn.

Tagger wasn't exactly sure how to clean the fish, even though she'd watched Miss Devlin do it many times. She felt she was wasting a lot of the white meat as she filleted it from the bone, but she still managed to thread two nice pieces on a stick she would use as a skewer. With the stick suspended between two forked, branches which she stuck in the ground, she could turn the fish slabs as they cooked.

Soon the pungent aroma of the fillets filled her nostrils. She could hardly wait for them to be done.

When the fish was browned and slightly crisp, Tagger pulled the two fillets from the skewer and carefully placed them on the china plate she'd brought. She sat back against a log and began to savor the bites of white, juicy meat. The fish was slightly oily, but still the most delicious food she'd ever eaten.

Wonderful ideas come to people at the most strange and unexpected times. Maybe it was because the fish had eased her hunger or maybe it was just because the fire felt so warm and comforting, but Tagger had just such an idea.

What if she were to catch more fish and trade them for other items she needed! People with goods often bartered or sold them for other goods. She could get the coins to pass the bridge and find her old home. Maybe someday she could even start a business. She smiled to herself. Now she was being silly.

But deep down, she knew it really could work. She could have a business. It wouldn't be easy for a girl, but it could be done. She'd have to work hard. She would certainly have to work hard. Maybe, just maybe.

And if she couldn't find Nana, if Nana was only a dream, or if she'd moved or died—as she feared she might have after all this time—Tagger would have the money she needed to live. In any case, she would not go back to Miss Devlin's. Never!

The townspeople who owned businesses, always seemed to be busy scribbling numbers and words on paper. Tagger couldn't read or write and that was a problem. But her biggest problem was that she was alone, and she was sure the village wouldn't allow it. No one had discovered it yet, but how long could it last?

CHAPTER 8
The Old Woman

It was late in the afternoon now, and Tagger felt satisfied after the delicious meal. The sun was dropping slowly into the western sky. A short nap sounded like a perfect way to end the day, but something made her keep pushing. She couldn't rest now, not when she had important matters on her mind. So she cleaned up the remains of her meal and headed up the river to the harbor where the boats would be returning to shore.

Her mind was filled with big thoughts. As she neared the harbor in the dwindling sunlight, she saw fishermen in sailboats and rowboats returning to the village after a hard day's work. Their little boats, scattered across the harbor, all coming in the same direction, looked to her like cows coming home to be milked.

The lot of the fishermen was a hard one. They usually worked long days, which often began before dawn. Tagger watched with interest now as they came in and unloaded the trawls, lines and catches from their boats. Those without boats still tended their lines, which were set along the edges of the piers and sea walls. They hoped to add a bit to their catches before dusk.

No one paid much attention to Tagger. All the fishermen were busy finishing up for the day, anxious to get home to their families and supper. When Tagger tried to ask them questions about fishing, they either ignored her or just pushed her out of the way.

One large, burly fisherman with a thatch of dark, oily hair, shoved her roughly aside and shouted, "Go away, you little ragamuffin. Leave us alone."

Tagger's feelings were hurt, but she wasn't surprised. No one ever seemed to take her seriously; they always saw her as a nuisance. But she didn't give up; she needed information. She knew there must be someone who would talk to her and listen to her plans.

As she quietly followed the fishermen about, Tagger noticed one grizzled old man at the edge of a fishing pier. He seemed different from the rest.

He was dressed in men's fishing clothes and the traditional yellow, wide-brimmed hat . . . but as she drew closer, she wondered, could it be? Yes, it was a woman!

When she peered closer into her face, Tagger saw that the woman was somewhat younger than she first appeared. Her haggard appearance was undoubtedly due to a hard life of long days on the water in the beating sun.

Tagger watched as the old woman intently went about her business. She held a net in her red, hardened hands, and dragged it expertly through the water as though she'd done it a thousand times before.

There were also three long, tattered lines dangling from the pier. The old lady kept an eye on them too while she tended her net.

With this particular drag of the net, the old woman entrapped about a half-dozen small, striped silver fish that were performing a most incredible show of flipping and twisting. Tagger was taking it all in, as the old lady freed the fish and threw them into a fish cart.

Peering into the cart, Tagger was excited to see that some of the old lady's fish were just like the one she caught!

"Excuse me, ma'am. Would you please tell me what kind of fish these are—the bluish-green ones?"

"Now, why would you care what kind they are," the woman muttered, without looking up.

"Because I caught one just like it today and ate it for noonday dinner," Tagger replied proudly. "I just wanted to know what they're called."

This triggered some interest in the woman, and she raised up stiffly to look at Tagger. For a moment, her eyes widened, almost imperceptibly as she stared at her. And then she squinted and blinked her eyes several times in an attempt to see her better. She obviously had a vision problem and probably needed spectacles.

Finally she said with a "humpf," "How could a little tyke like you catch a fish, 'specially this kind? Why, you're just a baby and those fish can be mean."

Frowning slightly, Tagger stood up straight and replied, "I take care of myself, and I can do more than you think."

"Where are your parents, and why aren't you in school, little boy?" the woman persisted.

Tagger was determined to be firm. "My pa's sick; we just got to town and he can't work yet, not until he gets well." Again, the pretended father with the mysterious illness, providing a shield of protection from the truth.

The woman considered all this for a moment, and then displaying the first signs of concern, she said, "That's too bad." But fearing she'd already said too much, she caught herself and added quickly, "That's none of my business, though. Now be off with you, I have work to do."

Tagger held her ground, watching the woman haul in her net again. After a few moments, when the woman had finished pulling the flopping fish from the net and dumping them into the fish cart, Tagger once again asked her the name of the blue-green fish.

"Well, it's not much of a surprise; they're called bluefish," she answered finally. "They're called snappers when they're young; they're a mean fish and often feed in a frenzy, but they're good fish to eat. Watch out when you catch one; they'll try to bite you even after you land 'em."

"How do you catch them?" Tagger asked, pressing the old woman for more details. "What type of bait do you use? Do you catch them on hooks as well as with nets? What do . . .?"

"Now hold on, boy, you're asking me questions quicker than I can answer them," the woman laughed impatiently. "I use bits of cut-up fish on the hooks and . . .."

As she spoke, a small bluefish jumped off the top of her fish cart and escaped into the lapping waves. This made her irritable, and she snapped, "Oh rats, I don't have time for idle chit-chat." She turned her back to Tagger and began packing up her gear.

But Tagger wasn't disappointed; she'd learned a great deal. Reluctantly she left the woman to her work, but as she turned to walk away, she called out, "I'll see you again, ma'am. Thank you."

When Tagger tried to sleep that night, she was filled with thoughts of the past. It was at times like this that she wondered who her real family was; what had they done for a living; what had they taught her in her early years that made her think and act the way she did? Did she even have a father?

Even if she could get across the river to the village of Mystic Bridge, she couldn't remember Nana's last name, what the house had looked like, where they lived or what the name of the lane was where it was located. And they'd probably already moved away by now. No, her dream of finding Nana was dimming.

CHAPTER 9
Gina

The clay pot, snug in Tagger's "cooling box," held four fat, lively night crawlers. But when Tagger awoke, she didn't rush off with it as she had the day before. Instead, she sat by the circle of stones that formed the boundary of her outdoor fireplace and thought about the possibilities that lay before her.

The thought for the day was fish. What was the best way for her to catch them? It was clear from her trip to the harbor that nets brought in the best catches, but it would take her a long time to make one.

She could probably fashion a crude net out of vines or bits of string, but that could take days or even weeks. And the next question was—would anyone buy her fish if she could catch them?

Finally she decided it would be best to use the hook and line again, and then see if she could find someone to buy her fish. If she could, she'd save her money until she had enough to buy a net. This project would require a lot of time and some careful planning. But she knew she could do it.

After she decided her best bet was to continue with the hook and line, she hopped to her feet, ready for action. She grabbed the clay pot, the battered bucket she used for drinking water, and a length of rope she'd found in the trash behind the boatyard. She planned to put her fish in the bucket so she could keep them fresh longer.

When she reached the deserted pier, it was again bathed in sunshine. She could feel the heat of the boards through her thin boots. The wind was stronger today and tossed the waves against the pilings. Pillows of foam bumped rhythmically along the length of the pier and the shoreline.

Tagger was afraid the rough waters would scare away the fish, but she was wrong. Not long after she dropped the hook in the water, there was a powerful hit on the bait. After she'd set the hook, the fish rose up out of the water, and she could see it was another bluefish.

She had to struggle with the fish for several minutes as it tested her patience and her strength. When it cut back beneath the pier and became entangled in a splintered piling, she thought for sure she'd lost it. But she was patient and determined and finally won out.

With a gasp of relief, she dragged the fish over the edge of the pier. It wasn't as large as the one the day before, but it was full of life.

While it performed its frenzied dance across the planks, wearing itself out, she quickly lowered the bucket into the water. With the rope tied to the bale, she was able to fill it about halfway before she pulled it up. The fish barely fit in the dented bucket, but the cool water calmed it enough that it slowed its wild flipping.

Tagger couldn't believe her luck. She was sure she'd triple her catch by midafternoon. But as the day wore on and she sat there, staring at a lifeless line, she became less hopeful. She had several bites, but no solid strikes. Gradually her bait disappeared. She had only about half a worm left on her hook when threatening black clouds blew across the sun.

Cold raindrops began to spot the weathered boards of the pier, and the skies darkened. The wind picked up and swept across the sound, swirling the ocean water in its path and whipping it into whitecaps.

Tagger felt the cool, wet breeze lift her hair and cool the nape of her neck. She grabbed up her hook and line and the bucket and raced for the shelter of the trees.

It was late afternoon, and while Tagger waited out the storm, she checked on her fish. It had died, but its color was good, and it still looked fresh.

Fortunately the shower was short-lived and as the sun peeped, then exploded through the parting clouds, Tagger headed for the village. She liked this time after a storm; everything seemed so clean and fresh.

As luck would have it, she saw the old woman from the day before. She was folding her net and coiling lines near the harbor.

Tagger hurried up, carrying the heavy bucket in front of her with both hands. It was swinging back and forth with each step, splashing out water.

"Hello, ma'am," she called out gleefully, "May I ask you a question?"

The old woman turned to look at Tagger and said, "Oh, the little fisherman. Be off with now—don't pester me. I have work to do."

"Please, ma'am, just one question. Look, I have a fish," she said as she thrust the bucket toward the old woman. She was fairly bursting with pride. "Could you just tell me how much I could sell it for in town."

The weathered eyes and wrinkled mouth softened just a

little from their automatic scowl. The old woman peered into the bucket.

"Yes, that's definitely a bluefish, but it won't be easy to sell," she said honestly. "Most of the shop owners buy from the same fishermen they've known for years, but if you could find someone to buy it, you should ask for half a cent per pound. That's the going rate. I'd say that fish is over three pounds, so charge one and a half cents."

"Thanks, ma'am," Tagger beamed.

"Let me get back to my work now," the woman snapped, but then she had a change of heart. "Good luck, little fisherman."

Tagger smiled to herself as she hurried off. "Just call me Tagger," she shouted back.

The village of Portersville was alive with activity at this hour. Women bustled about from shop to shop selecting foods for the evening meal, while their children scampered in and out among the tables and counters.

Everyone was so busy that Tagger was a little dazed by the confusion. She knew she was going to have to pull herself together if she was going to sell her fish. She straightened to her full height, pushed her damp hair back from her face, smoothed her shirt and "hiked up" her britches.

When she'd summoned all the courage she could muster, she went into a butcher shop she'd seen on Main Street. After a moment or two, she wiggled through the shoppers up to the counter. She'd heard a customer call the burly butcher, Sam, and saw that he was wrapping four fat pork cuts in a package for a tall, slim lady dressed in a long dress and white bonnet.

When Tagger finally caught Sam's eye, she spoke up firmly, "Mr. Sam, sir, I have a fresh bluefish here that I'd like to sell you for one and a half cents." Her eyes were pleading and her voice wavered slightly.

When the butcher saw Tagger's old clothing and battered bucket, he yelled at her, "Get out of my shop. I'd never buy fish from an urchin. If you don't leave right now, I'll call the sheriff."

Tagger knew there was no point in arguing. She shrugged her shoulders, embarrassed by the assault of words, and walked slowly out the door. She was disappointed but not defeated.

There was another butcher shop across town—Derek Meats, but the reaction from the owner was the same. She was humiliated in front of the other customers and, by now, totally disheartened. She thought there were probably other butcher shops in Mystic Bridge, but she had no way to get across the river.

She decided to give up for the day. Dusk was falling, with the kind of pearlish color that casts a pale, eerie glow. Just what she needed to remind her that today had been a failure. To make matters worse, she saw a commotion down the street.

There was a group of children, two boys and a girl, gathered outside a meat store on the next cross street called Water Street. The children were nicely dressed, but they were behaving like little hooligans. The taller of the two boys and the girl were throwing mud balls at the window of the shop, and the younger boy shouted ugly remarks at the lady owner inside.

"Fat, old pig!" "Whale blubber!" The stinging words flew from his flushed face like bullets.

Tagger couldn't believe anyone could be that cruel. She immediately set down her bucket and ran up to the boy who'd been shouting.

"Shame on you," Tagger scolded, as she grabbed his arm. She was bigger than all the children. Although the boy managed to jerk his arm away, he realized he was no match for Tagger.

"Leave me alone," he screamed petulantly. "You ain't my pa." The boy was fuming, and his face was red. Tagger waited until his temper subsided, and then she caught him by the arm again.

"You're very cruel to insult this poor lady." Tagger could see through the shop window that the woman was weeping. "See, you've made her cry. Now, you and your friends apologize."

The children knew they had no choice. Tagger led them over to the shop, and they each sullenly said he or she was sorry. Their heads were bowed as they shuffled off, but just as they rounded the corner, the older boy shook his fist at Tagger and ran off.

Tagger went into the shop. "Are you all right, ma'am?" she asked softly. She was afraid to meet the woman's gaze directly, ever fearful that she might be detected.

The portly store owner was still sobbing, but she managed a smile. "Yes, I'm fine," she sniffed. "Thank you. That was very brave of you to run those naughty children off."

"Why were they so mean to you?" Tagger asked.

"They love to make fun of me because I'm large, and they know it hurts me. I never treat them badly, I love children, but they always want to hurt me—I guess because I'm different."

When the woman had stopped crying, Tagger could see

she had a lovely, compassionate face. Her curly, dark hair was cut short around her face, framing her gentle brown eyes. She wore a blue gingham dress and a white apron, both of which were clean and starched.

As Tagger looked over the lady's store, she saw that this was the best selection of meat she'd seen so far. But, to her surprise, there were no customers.

"You look pretty hungry," the lady said. "Why don't you let me cook you some food. That's the least I can do."

"Oh no, I can't accept. I've done nothing special. Besides I have my own fish that I've been trying to sell."

"I'll be glad to buy it from you, young man," said the lady. "Where is it?"

Suddenly Tagger remembered she'd left the fish in the street and ran off to get it. When she returned to the shop, she told the lady the price was one and a half cents. Without a word, the lady went to the ornate cash register, rang up "no sale," and returned with three, half-cent coins.

Tagger started to reach for the fish, but she was crushed when she saw it. It had turned a sickening lighter color and the fresh look was gone.

It was painful for her, but she knew she had to tell the kind lady she couldn't sell her the fish. She couldn't take a chance on selling her something that wasn't acceptable.

"You're very honest and kind, young man," the woman said gently. "What's your name?"

"Tagger," she replied enthusiastically, hoping she was making a new friend.

"My name's Gina," the woman said. "Please come back whenever you have more fish, Tagger, and I'll be happy to buy them from you."

"Thank you," said Tagger. "I'm sure I'll see you again.

Goodbye." Tagger knew Gina was sincere; she trusted her instantly.

It was almost dark as Tagger walked back through the village and then crossed the woods to her cottage. Halfway home, the odor from the bucket told her the fish had spoiled. She stopped and threw it into the woods beside the path.

The rest of the walk home was a little more tiring, because she had neither money nor the fish. But her long day's work hadn't been in vain, for now she had someone who would buy her fish when she caught them. She'd been nearly ready to give up; now she had hope.

When she returned to the cottage, her heart sank. A woman was sitting on a stump near the door; she called out as Tagger approached. "Hello, are you the new boy in town, Tagger?"

"Yes I am," Tagger replied. "Greetings to you, ma'am." She'd already rehearsed what she'd say if anyone ever came to check on her and her "pa."

The lady introduced herself as Mrs. Priscilla Anderson, the sheriff's wife. "I heard your pa was feeling poorly. I just wanted to see if there was anything I could do, but no one was home. Has anyone from the church come to call, yet?"

"No," Tagger said, "but we don't need any help. Pa has the ague. He caught it when he was sailing in the South Seas. Sometimes he has a fever and feels real bad, but he felt a little better today. I think he went out to hunt."

"Oh my, a South Seas ague! That sounds fearsome," Mrs. Anderson said. "Is it catching?"

"Pa doesn't know," Tagger continued the lie, "but he always makes sure that we don't eat from the same dish or drink from the same cup." Perhaps she might forestall future questions if folks thought he was contagious.

Mrs. Anderson looked concerned, "Well tell him I was here to pay a visit, and that perhaps I can meet him soon." She started to leave, but then she remembered the basket she'd set down beside the stump.

"Here, dear," she said offering the basket to Tagger. "I brought you and your father some corned beef and potatoes left over from dinner. You can return the basket when I see you the next time."

After Tagger had thanked her, Mrs. Anderson left down the same path she'd come. Tagger breathed a sigh of relief; she'd escaped the questions this time, but how about the next time? Right now, she was just going to enjoy that corned beef.

CHAPTER 10
The Investment

The first day after she met Gina, she caught just one fish. It was another bluefish, but it was larger and even feistier. She had quite a time landing it, and it snapped at her every time she moved near it.

This time she made it to the village before the fish spoiled. Gina was glad to see Tagger and only too happy to buy the fish from her. She would have paid her more than the two cents Tagger wanted, but she knew Tagger's pride wouldn't allow her to accept more.

When Gina gave her the pennies for her fish, Tagger was thrilled. This was the first money she'd ever earned on her own.

Once Tagger had seen the miserly town baker at Groton caress and fondle his money as though it were a pet. She knew instinctively this kind of passion for money was wrong. Money was only valuable in terms of what it could buy, and she had a plan for these coins.

Gina seemed so delighted to have a visitor that Tagger agreed to stay a while for tea. They climbed the wooden staircase at the back of the store. It took them upstairs to where Gina had a little apartment. Tagger could see right away that she was an excellent housekeeper.

The kitchen was spotless as well as bright and cozy. A

wood-burning Franklin stove puffed away in the corner, warming the teakettle for the tea. Gina motioned for Tagger to sit at the oak table, which was surrounded by four comfortable chairs. The table was covered with a red and white checked cloth, made of the same material as the frilly curtains hung at the little windows above the dry sink.

Adjacent to the kitchen was a small living room with a homey feel. There was a comfortable-looking brown settee against the long wall and two matching armchairs on each side of the brick fireplace. The hardwood floor was covered with a handmade, braided rug of many colors and fabrics.

"Oh Gina, what a beautiful rug! Did you make it?" Tagger asked, clearly impressed by Gina's creativity.

"Yes I did, Tagger. Thank you." Gina glowed pink from the compliment.

A large oil painting of a majestic sailing ship hung on the wall behind the couch, and a portrait of a handsome elderly couple was above the fireplace.

"Those were my dear parents, Philip and Hannah," Gina explained, when she saw Tagger's glance fall on the portrait. "I miss them very much. Mama passed away three years ago and Papa followed her six months later. They were such a happy couple. In some ways it was good they passed away so close together because Papa didn't have to live long without Mama. But it was so hard for me."

"I'm sure it was. I'm so sorry, Gina," Tagger said.

While they sat in the kitchen, sipping hot, orange-pekoe tea, Gina told Tagger a little about herself. When her father had died, she was the only survivor. A local attorney advised her to sell the butcher shop and use the money to open a sundries or notions shop, something that he thought would be more suitable for a woman. But she'd spent her life in her dad's butcher shop, McGuire's, and wanted to continue in his footsteps, so she kept the shop and ran it herself.

She was very proud of her father, as he had been of her. Throughout the years he had taught her everything he knew about butchering and running a business.

"You know, Tagger, I learned a lot from Papa—how to cut meat, how to trim the fat, how to price the cuts. But the thing I remember most is that my father always wanted to sell the best quality of meat.

"Papa would tell me over and over, 'Gina, sell your customers the best fish, roasts and chops you can find. If you do that, you'll always stay in business.'"

When she reopened the store after her father's death, Gina had spent a great deal of time talking to the local meat producers and fishermen. Following Papa's advice, she constantly looked for the best meat and sold it for the best prices. She prided herself on her merchandise. Everybody liked her; she was fair to her customers, and she insisted on selling only the best.

Her father's rule had sunk in. Soon her business began to grow and everyone started coming to Gina's. But to her surprise, the other butchers became jealous. Instead of competing honestly with her, they just banded together and tried to think of ways to hurt her business.

First they started concocting ridiculous rumors to discourage her customers. They said she was selling horsemeat for beef, and then they said she wasn't properly icing down the seafood and meat to keep it fresh. For a long time, no one believed the rumors because Gina was so well liked by the townspeople.

Finally, her rivals came up with the cruelest idea of all. They tried to make the villagers believe she had a strange infirmity that caused her to gain weight. They said the disease could pass from her to the cuts of meat she handled, and anyone buying it would be affected in the same way.

Most of the villagers knew this couldn't be true, but the rumors continued. Soon her business began dropping off.

And then one day a little boy choked on a chicken bone and died. It was a terrible accident and had nothing to do with Gina. But when it was learned that the boy's mother had bought the chicken from Gina's shop, the word spread far and wide that her food was indeed contaminated.

Little by little, her customers dropped to only a few. She had enough business to give her an income that would cover the basics, but every day was a struggle to make ends meet.

Tagger listened sympathetically to the sad story that Gina told and then shared a little about her situation. She trusted Gina, but she continued the story she had fabricated about her sick father. The truth was just too much to risk.

Despite her own meager income, Gina wanted to help this precocious little boy who was perched on the oak chair in her kitchen. Her heart went out to him.

But again Tagger refused any help. "I only ask that you buy my fish," she said, "that is, if you think they're good enough for your customers."

"Of course I will," Gina replied. They had an agreement.

The conversation turned to fishing, and Tagger mentioned to Gina that she needed more fishing supplies, but she wasn't sure where to get them. Gina immediately recommended Markle's Mercantile. Mr. Markle seemed to be a fair man, and he sold a variety of good supplies and equipment.

As soon as she said her goodbyes and thanked Gina for the tea, Tagger headed straight for Markle's. She held the coins in her hand as she walked through the gravel streets of the town. She had money now, but it wasn't enough to cross the bridge yet. She would just have to use it to make more.

A tingle of excitement swept through her as she pushed the brass door handle. When she found the fishing section of the store, she was awed by the variety of nets, poles, sinkers, hooks and lines that Mr. Markle carried. How would she ever be able to make a selection of what she needed?

She guessed the man behind the counter to be Mr. Markle. He didn't run her off when she walked into the store like the other store owners had, but he watched her closely as she wandered among the shelves.

Finally, she took a chance and went to the counter. With confidence she didn't really feel, she stated firmly, "I'd like to buy a fishing line and a hook." Her voice wasn't nearly as loud as she'd hoped, but he had heard her, because he looked up from his paperwork.

"Oh you would, would you?" said the man with a slight smile. "And do you have any money?"

"Yes," Tagger replied proudly and showed him the two pennies. Despite his gruff words, she liked this man. He had snow-white hair and a wrinkled face that looked as though it had been carved from hardening clay. The little smile puckered the corners of his eyes.

He helped her pick out a line made of twisted cotton and a hook especially designed for catching saltwater fish. The cost was exactly two cents.

Just as she was leaving, a man and a woman walked in together. The woman was Mrs. Anderson and she guessed the tall, handsome man with her to be the sheriff. "Hello, Tagger," Priscilla Anderson said cheerfully. "How is your pa doing?"

Tagger was caught off guard, but she managed to think of a quick response. "He's not doing too well, the fever has him down again. I'm just trying to let him rest until he's better."

"I'm sorry to hear that, Tagger. Tell him we're all praying for him."

"Thank you, Mrs. Anderson, I will," she said as she quickly made her way to the door. Sheriff Anderson watched her, but didn't speak. He only nodded as his wife told her good night.

When she reached her cottage later, the early summer sun was sinking through the trees, turning everything a rosy glow. How she loved this time of day. "I know I can make it," she told herself. All she needed was time to carry out her plans. She was certain she'd soon be catching enough fish to feed herself and earn enough money to cross the bridge to find Nana—that was what she had come here to do, wasn't it?

In the days that followed, Tagger went to the lodging house once a week and scrubbed the floor. Betty gave her two loaves of bread each time she came, and they began to stretch farther now, because she had fish to go with them.

CHAPTER 11
The Tagger Pouch

The Connecticut coast was enjoying the best days of summer now, and the days were warm and breezy. Tagger was beginning to collect quite an array of hooks and lines and sinkers. She was still saving to buy a net.

It had become too warm to wear the long cloak with the many pockets, so Tagger thought about making something she could use to carry all her small items—even the few coins she was collecting.

One night after dinner, she pulled out the old sewing kit Nana had given her so long ago. With a small piece of muslin she'd bought at the general store, she began to fashion a pocket that had a flap over it. The flap had a hook and eye, so it could be closed securely to keep items from falling out. The pocket measured about five inches wide and six inches deep and was just the right size to hold all of Tagger's personal belongings.

Next she attached a long strip of material to the top and back of the pocket and sewed a buttonhole into this piece. Then she sewed a button onto the inside of the waistband of her britches in the front. In this manner she could attach the pocket to the front of her britches where it was convenient to use. This freed her hands too, so that she didn't have to worry about the location of her valuable items while she worked. Tagger was proud of her little invention and called it the "tagger pouch." The next time she went into Mr.

Markle's store, he noticed the handy little pouch and asked where she'd gotten it.

When she told him she'd made the tagger pouch herself, Mr. Markle was quite impressed, "Well Tagger, that's a mighty fine idea you got there. How about making some more? I can sell them here in the store for you."

Gina was excited for Tagger when she told her about the deal with Mr. Markle and agreed to help her make them.

Gina never failed to marvel at Tagger. What an inventive and hard-working little boy he was! But how had he learned to sew so well? Tagger explained to Gina that when his mother had become ill, she'd taught him many household tasks, so that he would be able to take care of his father if she passed away. She had lovingly passed on many skills to Tagger before her early death at the age of thirty. The story was growing. It wasn't really lying. Didn't they call this self preservation?

During the day Tagger fished. Some days she'd catch two or three fish, but ever so often she would only catch one. When she caught only one fish, she'd always sell it to Gina, even if it meant going without her dinner. It was important to save all the money she could for crossing that bridge—or for the ominous winter, sure to come.

Most of the time she caught bluefish and striped bass, but one day, she caught something completely different. It was about the same size as a smaller bluefish, but it was a flat fish with a spotted, brownish topside and a totally white belly. Its top and bottom fins ran almost the length of its body. But the most remarkable thing about this fish was its eyes. They were both on top of its head.

When she ran into the old fisherwoman that day on her way to town, she asked what kind of fish this was. The old

woman was surprised when she looked into the bucket. "Why that's a winter flounder. Some folks call 'em flukes. You're in for some mighty fine eating. You were lucky to catch him. They start heading out to sea about this time of year. You must be a good fisherman, indeed."

Suddenly the old woman stopped herself, fearful she'd been too friendly and said too much. She dropped her head and started down the path.

"Please don't go yet," Tagger pleaded. "Can you tell me about the fish's eyes? Are they all like that?"

"When those critters are born, they got eyes on both sides of their head," the old woman explained, "but as they get older, the eyes slide 'round to the right side. They start to feed off the bottom then. That way they can look up at their food. There's a summer flounder too. Their eyes slide round to the left. I gotta go now. I got work to do." With that, the old woman trudged off before Tagger could say anymore.

"I don't know your name," Tagger called after her. There was no answer.

Gradually Tagger increased her catches, and her garden was starting to come up. She had lettuce, onions, peas, green beans and carrots. And it wouldn't be long before she could harvest her potatoes and squash. She had food to eat and was even managing to save a little money from the sale of her fish.

Tagger continued her visits to the lodging house each Saturday evening to scrub the floor or clean out the fireplace, in return for bread. She still needed bread in her diet, and it was just too expensive to buy, so she appreciated this opportunity to earn it.

When she had been out exploring one day, Tagger had walked to the big, wooden drawbridge that connected Portersville to the village on the east side of the Mystic River, Mystic Bridge. She had learned how much it would be to cross on foot. Now that she had the money and had mustered the courage to do so, she thought she should try to find her family.

The day of her trip to her hometown started hopefully enough. It was a bright, sunny day and the water reflected sparkles of light as she walked across the drawbridge. But her eagerness faded as she wandered around the village.

Mystic Bridge was a pleasant little community, but no one looked as though they might be related to her. She couldn't find the house where she had lived, nor did any of the lanes look familiar. She thought vaguely that she had been here before, but nothing triggered any special memories. No, she was sure her family was gone now; they'd undoubtedly moved away and left her to fend for herself.

Though she was disappointed, it was worth the precious money she'd spent to finally prove that she had no family. She would go on with her life on her own. Maybe that was what she had really wanted afterall. So far the town had left her alone. Maybe they would forever.

Once Tagger had bought enough fishing supplies to get by, she began to spend some of her profits for other necessities. She bought corn meal, salt, dried milk, and soap, but she hesitated to spend too much on what she considered "luxuries," like clothes, shoes and furniture.

The old fisherwoman, whose name she fianlly learned was Mary, taught her how to salt down and dry her fish. This was a big help because now she could stockpile some of the larger fillets for later.

CHAPTER 12
John

The next day after her trip to Mystic Bridge, Tagger had a particularly successful time on the pier. She'd sold four fish to Gina and wanted to celebrate in some small way. She felt she'd earned it.

Her mind was spinning with ideas for improving her catches as she walked along the gravel streets of Portersville. She only half-saw the quaint shops, still crowded with customers shopping for last-minute items before closing.

She had a single-minded purpose tonight and headed straight for the brass shop. The shop had already closed for the day, as was announced by the red and white "closed" sign dangling on a cord inside the door. The only light came from a nearby street lamp.

This was such an important moment to her. She was always captivated by the array of brass fittings, hinges and assorted hardware items. But her eyes went right to the brass doorknobs.

They were beautiful. Some of them had molded sculptures. Others were so smooth and shiny that she could see her reflection in them.

There was one particular doorknob she longed to own. It was oval-shaped, with a raised diamond decoration on the front. In the center was a black enamel circle that shone like a jewel.

Whenever she gazed at it, she thought of grander things, of better times. There was something about it that triggered her dreams—dreams of a spacious, ivy-covered cottage, with green shutters, and, of course, the oval doorknob on the front door.

Somehow she believed this simple object held a special meaning for her—a meaning she couldn't quite explain. Whatever it was, it gave her a reason to keep going. It kept her striving for something better—and sticking it out when things got tough.

As she stood there, enchanted by the beautiful doorknob, she sensed someone behind her. She turned abruptly to see a handsome boy standing there. He was a few years older than she and had a slim, strong build. His eyes were brown, bright and searching. A few strands of his dark hair fell lightly across his broad forehead.

She always noticed people's eyes. She'd once heard the eyes were the windows to the soul, and she felt as though she was looking right into the boy's soul as they stood there. His mouth was full and gentle with a slight upward turn at the corners.

Tagger looked so serious that he broke into a broad smile. "Did I frighten you?" he asked, grinning.

"No," Tagger blushed deeply and lowered her head slightly, so he wouldn't see her girlish face plainly. "I guess I was just daydreaming. I didn't realize you were there. Who are you?" she said in her best imitation of a male voice.

"My name's John. I was just passing through the village when I saw you standing here, staring at the brass fixtures."

Tagger smiled warmly. She noticed that his clothes were as tattered as hers. His shoes were made from crudely fashioned strips of leather. As they talked, she wasn't surprised to learn that he was alone too. His parents had died two years ago from consumption, the dreaded lung disease.

He went on to say that he was on his way to Mystic Bridge, because he'd heard he could find work there. He wanted to work on a fishing boat or maybe a coastal packet.

"I hope you find what you want, John. My name's Tagger." She didn't tell him that she was alone too.

"Now, I must know, lad," he said seriously. "Why have you been staring at the brass fixtures? Is there one you fancy?"

"Yes, see the brass doorknob, the one in the back row? It has the diamond and a black circle on it. Well, I know this sounds just plain silly, but when I stare at it, it seems to sweep me away—to another time and another place. I can't explain it. Someday I'd like to have a big cottage with a doorknob just like that one. I think dreams are important. Don't you?"

"Of course," he agreed smiling. "I want to wish you the best of luck, but I don't think you'll be needing it. You're the kind of boy who'll find what he wants.

"Goodbye for now, Tagger," he waved as he started across the village green. He shifted his small knapsack to his other shoulder and sauntered off on his own adventure.

She was sorry to see him go. Maybe they could have been friends. "Goodbye," she called after him.

CHAPTER 13
The Schoolhouse

The children came from every direction. Some of them ran, some skipped, and some just shuffled along the dusty path to the clearing. They were all going to the same place—the old schoolhouse. The weathered building seemed to stand proudly in the morning glow, even after all its years of service—ready to welcome Portersville's children. It was the first day of the midsummer session. Children would study until the harvest and then go to work with their parents until late in the fall.

The older children pretended to be disinterested in returning to school, so they walked slowly, trying to look sophisticated and slightly sullen. But the younger ones were delighted to be together again. They had so many stories to tell each other. A general babble of childish sounds filled the air.

A tall boy named Joe, who was sporting a new indigo-dyed flaxen shirt and navy blue trousers, was trying gamely to juggle three large green apples. His intent was to impress two young girls standing nearby. The girls twisted their braids in unison as they watched and giggled delightedly.

Suddenly Joe lost control and the apples flew everywhere. One rolled right up to the booted foot of the stern schoolmaster, Mr. Jensen. He had just sauntered out of the schoolhouse to see if he could bring order to the mêlée.

The schoolmaster stared first at the apple and then at Joe. "Is this for me?" he asked, with a stony glare. Joe nodded dumbly, afraid to say anything that would get him into more trouble.

Tagger watched all this from a distance, under the low branches of a large oak tree. She was trying to assess the situation without appearing conspicuous.

Regardless of age, the boys wore basically the same type of clothes, heavy dark pants or britches, long-sleeved cotton or linen shirts and either felt caps or straw hats. Tagger guessed that many of the pants and shirts were brand new, because the boys seemed uncomfortable and frequently scratched at the stiff cloth.

The girls, on the other hand, seemed to be perfectly comfortable in their new dresses or skirts and blouses. The skirts reached almost to the ground and covered white petticoats that peeped out when they walked. Tagger guessed that their mothers had made them themselves with loving care.

Most of the girls wore braids and nearly all of them had bright bonnets that made up a rainbow of colors. Everyone but Tagger carried dinner pails, and she just knew they would be packed with all kinds of tasty goodies.

Yes, Tagger was definitely out of place. Although her clothing was freshly washed, she still wore the old white shirt and the same ill-fitting britches she'd found in the inn. Her hat was pulled low over her eyes.

Taking her own little survey of the children in the schoolyard, she noticed that a few of them were smaller than she; most were larger. This confirmed what she had guessed, that she was about in the middle of the students age-wise; probably more than nine by now.

Tagger had heard children in the village talking about school starting today, and she knew she had to try to go too. There would never be any hope of seeing her dreams come true unless she received some schooling.

Undoubtedly the children would tease her, and she would feel left out, but it was a small price to pay if she could learn something useful. She would try the " sick papa" story here too. Now here she was waiting to see how it would all unfold.

The schoolmaster was a serious, distinguished man, lean and wiry. It seemed that a smile might crack his face. He had thin, tight lips, and his cool gray eyes heightened his look of intelligence, but made him seem totally unapproachable.

He was trying to maintain a sense of decorum among the rollicking children by solemnly ringing a long-handled bell. It was time for school to begin.

A few of the teenagers lingered a while, savoring one last moment of freedom, but the giggly youngsters were anxious to get started, some of them for the first time. They quickly formed a disorderly line and bumped and shoved their way into the classroom.

As he was about to close the door on the last straggler, the schoolmaster glanced up and spotted Tagger. She had moved shyly to the edge of the walkway.

After staring for a moment, he recovered quickly. "You can't come in here dressed like that, young man. I can't imagine why your parents would let you come to school looking like that. Have your parents signed your enrollment papers and paid the book fee?" Tagger shook her head mutely.

"I didn't know we had a new student in town, " he continued. "Who are your parents? I really must talk to them. Where do you live?"

Tagger was crushed and frightened. Although she tried to fight them back, large teardrops welled up in her eyes, and she couldn't speak. She turned and ran down the dirt path, her vision blurred by tears, back to the sanctuary of the woods. As she ran, she could hear the jeers and snickers of the children and then the stern voice of the schoolmaster trying to reestablish order.

When she could no longer hear any sounds but the screams of the birds wheeling overhead, she slowed her pace to a walk. She was slumped over and out of breath, and then suddenly she became angry. She stamped her foot in the dusty path.

Why hadn't she spoken up to the schoolmaster, explained that these were the only clothes she had? Even though she didn't have fancy, well-made clothes like the other boys, she was clean and dressed decently. Maybe he would have understood and let her attend. But she was too upset now to go back.

What would she do? "If I don't go to school," she brooded, "I'll never have a life. I'll never have a chance for happiness."

Why was everything so hard for her? Why didn't she have parents like everyone else? Why hadn't her mother come back for her? Why had Nana gone away? It was easy to feel sorry for herself, but she'd realized long ago there was no point. It didn't make her feel any better, and no one seemed to care if she felt sorry for herself or not.

CHAPTER 14
Diane

The day after her disappointing experience at the schoolhouse, Tagger went to the pier as usual. A gentle breeze blew across the weathered boards and the sound was ablaze with the brilliance of light meeting water. She was ready for a big day, thinking of how she would use the new line she'd just bought.

The reflection from the waves was so bright that Tagger had trouble seeing at first, and then she realized, to her surprise, that someone else was there. Someone was on her pier!

It was a girl. She wore a long faded dress and an old black cape that was many sizes too large for her. Her long, straight brown hair fell like a curtain over her hands as she held them up to her face. When she heard the sound of footsteps, she looked up quickly. Tagger could see that she had small, rounded features and bright green eyes, and she was perhaps three or four years older than herself.

"Hello, my name is Tagger. Who are you?" Tagger asked.

"My name's Diane," she said quietly. It wasn't difficult for Tagger to see that she was distressed and apparently very hungry.

Diane pointed to a rise in the shoreline where several large, white pines were clustered around a mansion. "I live over there in the servants' quarters," she said slowly, watching

Tagger. "I see you fishing everyday, and I thought maybe you would give me a fish. You can't be eating all of the ones you're catching."

"Don't they feed you there?" Tagger asked, puzzled by the question.

"Yes, but not much. They never give me meat or fish— just bread and porridge," she replied.

Tagger's heart went out to her; she knew how frightening it was to be alone and hungry.

Everything was quiet except for the gentle lapping of the waves on the rocky shore. Tagger thought over her response. Finally she replied, "I could certainly give you a fish, Diane, but how about this? Why don't I let you use one of my lines? If you catch two fish, you may keep one for yourself. How does that sound to you?"

The girl thought a moment. "All right," Diane said resolutely. "Show me how to do it."

As they fished, Diane confided in Tagger. Diane and her family had lived in New London when she was born. One day her father had fallen in love with the idea of adventure and riches and had signed on with a sailing fleet bound for the coast of Florida. He never returned, and she and her mother had to survive on their own.

They both acquired jobs as servants at a large private residence in New London. The owner of the house, Mr. VanSanten, was a kind master and gave them a nice room in the back where they lived. He also provided them with generous meals.

They were content in this situation, until one day the house was stricken with cholera. The dreaded disease took the life of her mother and another servant, as well as the life of their dear master, Mr. VanSanten.

Diane didn't know what to do. She fled the disease-ridden house and headed to the Mystic River area, sleeping and eating wherever she could. One day, she found an abandoned boathouse and tried to live there. But the town authorities found her and made her live with the Braxton family, where she was now. She was bound out to them for four years until she was eighteen. It wouldn't have been so bad living there in the nice house, but they were very stingy people, particularly Mrs. Braxton. Diane had to work hard, cleaning the big house and doing the washing, but she and the other servants were fed poorly. She was always hungry and had no place to turn.

Tagger learned that Diane was only twelve, but her hard life made her look older than her years. She'd determined that she could shorten the time of her service by saying she was fourteen. That way, she only had to pass four years with the Braxtons instead of six.

As she listened to Diane's story, Tagger wondered if she could keep her true identity a secret until she was eighteen. She doubted it, because she knew that soon people would be asking about her father's health again.

How jubilant Diane was when she caught her first fish. Tagger was as excited as Diane and told her so.

"See, you can do it," Tagger encouraged her. Diane smiled back at her and for a moment, there was a bond between these two young girls, even though Diane thought Tagger was a boy.

But as soon as Diane caught her second fish, she ran off with it immediately—not even bothering to wrap it in anything to keep it fresh. Tagger was sure that fish was destined to be Diane's dinner.

Tagger also caught three plump bluefish herself that day. She planned to sell two of hers and Diane's smaller one to Gina.

"My, you have been busy today," exclaimed Gina, when she saw the catch. "How did you do it all by yourself?"

"Well, I didn't catch them all myself," Tagger explained. "I had some help from a girl who showed up on the pier today. I taught her to fish and told her she could have one fish if she caught two. She did, and she was so proud of herself. It made me feel good too."

"I'm sure it did. It's always good to pass on what you know to someone else." Gina stopped and thought for a moment. "I know of other poor children around this area who could use work like this."

"Yes, I suppose there are some," Tagger replied. She was passing the fish, one by one, to Gina, who laid them in the big ice chest.

"I see them everywhere begging for handouts," Gina continued, still on the same line of thought. "They're so sad, my heart goes out to them all. You know, Tagger, maybe you could hire them and pay them in fish, just like your new friend. That way you'd have someone to help you and keep you company. And they'd have a source of food."

Tagger suddenly saw the merit to this idea. What a wonderful plan! Everyone would benefit, and she would have someone to help her pass the long days on the pier. That is, if she continued to escape the authorities.

"Oh, Gina, you're right," Tagger was excited now, "but how can I let them know I'll hire them?"

"Leave that to me," Gina replied with confidence. "I'll have them at your pier tomorrow. You just teach them how to fish."

CHAPTER 15
The Others

The next day, Tagger lugged her lines, net, bucket and bait to the pier. Who would she find there? She tried to keep her emotions in check because she didn't want to be disappointed.

As she approached the weathered pier, she saw them. Just as Gina had promised.

There were two rag-tag boys on her pier; a tall, thin boy was sitting on the planks and a shorter, plumper boy slouched over the pilings. Both were gangly, fightened children—afraid to let anyone know they were scared and nervous too.

Tagger knew their lives were hard, so she decided right then and there she'd have to be patient and understanding. She'd start them out gradually and not expect too much the first day.

Clearing her throat and summoning all her strength, Tagger spoke. "My name's Tagger. I'm glad you came. Would you tell me your names?"

At first there was silence, and then the taller of the two stood up to his full height and said quietly, "I'm Edward." He seemed relieved to have it over with.

The shorter boy was next. "Hello," he said, tipping his hat to her. "I'm Renaud, pleased to make your acquaintance, Tagger."

After the introductions, Tagger gave them basic instructions about fishing. She showed them how to bait the hooks, how to throw their lines out from the pier, how to set the hook when a fish struck at the bait, how to land the fish, and how to take it off the hook. Tagger concluded that the boys were a little older than she, which made it a bit difficult for her to take a tutorial role.

Edward was withdrawn and seemingly resistant, but soon he could see she wanted the best for all of them. As the day wore on, he became more and more cooperative. Edward wore ragged pants that hit him at mid calf; the sleeves of his white cotton shirt were much too short. He pretended to be gruff and proud, but his eyes said otherwise. They were soft and sensitive, and Tagger was careful to be gentle with him.

Renaud had the best nature of the two. He was husky and muscular with an impish glint in his blue-gray eyes. He quickly overcame his distrust of Tagger and seemed interested in helping in any way he could. His only fault was clumsiness. He kept tangling his lines and catching his hook in the side of the pier.

"It makes me feel real good to do something useful," he told Tagger as he finally landed his first fish.

Tagger had to bite her lip to keep from laughing, because she knew he was sincere. Instead she nodded her head solemnly. He would be a good worker, as soon as he had a little experience.

About midday, Diane returned, surprised to find the others fishing with Tagger. The taste of the juicy bluefish had driven her back to the pier for more.

"Would it be all right if I fish for you again today?" Diane asked Tagger, as she looked around the pier. "Mrs. Braxton doesn't care what I do in the afternoons as long as all the work is finished in the morning."

"Of course," Tagger replied. "I'm glad you came back. I can

use your help." Now Tagger had a worthy crew of three young workers. She was pleased and proud.

The warmth from the afternoon sun began to fade and a cool breeze picked up. The complaining among the young fishermen increased the later it got, but they all knew they'd had quite a good day. They'd learned a great deal, and they were proud of their catches, but soon they were on their way home. Tagger was left to figure out how she would get her fish to market.

"Could you use some help, Tagger?" Renaud called out as he came out of the shadows at end of the pier. "It looks like you have more than you can handle. I'm going toward town too; I'll carry the bucket, if you like."

"Thank you, Renaud, I could use your help," she replied. "I'm going to Gina's butcher shop in the square. Is that close to where you're going?"

"Yes it is," Renaud answered.

As they walked along companionably, Tagger felt comfortable with Renaud. She felt a little safer, too, as darkness crept into the harbor.

They exchanged little tidbits of conversation on several neutral subjects, such as the weather and fishing. Renaud was a good conversationalist, and Tagger felt like she was getting to know him quickly. And then Tagger probed carefully, "What happened to your family, Renaud?"

There was a short pause, and then he began his sad story.

"My dad was a fishermen. He was buying his own boat, and sometimes he'd take me out in it. One day while I was in school, my parents took the boat over to Stonington to meet the ship bringing goods down from New York. On the way, their boat was struck by lightning and burned. They were both killed."

His shoulders drooped slightly at the weight of his sad story. "I'm so sorry. Renaud," Tagger said compassionately. "How did you ever deal with your loss?"

"I couldn't at first. I was only ten, and there was no one to help me. We didn't have any family in town. I ran away to Boston. I had to . . . had to learn to beg for my food. I hated doing that. My parents worked hard, and they were proud. I wanted to be like them and earn my own living, so eventually I returned here.

"When I arrived back in Portersville, the authorities saw me and realized I was the orphan boy who'd run away. They told me I would have to be put into service. So I was bound out to the blacksmith, Mr. Sharply. I live in the back of the shop on a cot. Mr. Sharply's a good man, but he doesn't have a wife or anyone to cook for him, so I don't have much to eat. I rise at dawn and I'm bound to serve him for only half a day. Then I can be on the pier in the afternoon."

Tagger had a new respect for Renaud. He had that sense of responsibility that just seemed to be born in some people.

"What about you, Tagger," Renaud asked now. "Where are your parents?"

Tagger instinctively knew she could trust Renaud, so she told him the truth. "I really don't know," she replied. "My mother left me at an inn when I was four, with a lady named Miss Devlin. When she left me, she said she'd come back, but she never did. Miss Devlin made me work in the inn with her. It wasn't so bad, but she wouldn't let me go to school or have friends. Finally, I ran away without pay or papers."

Then she told him the story of how she found the cottage and began catching fish, but not about her true identity as a girl. It was just too risky.

"You're a strong lad, Tagger. You've learned to take care of yourself," Renaud said with respect. "I liked the way you taught us to fish today. We need to stick together." He grinned his twinkling smile and said, "You know what they say: there's strength in numbers."

She nodded in agreement, happy to have another new friend. "Do you know why Edward is alone?"

"Edward confided in me one day that his father deserted his mother when she was pregnant with his sister," Renaud continued. "Edward tried to take care of his mother by doing small jobs at the livery stable next to the blacksmith shop where I work in Portersville. When it was time for his mother to have the baby, she died in childbirth, as did his sister. That left Edward all alone. He was only eight and the town fathers decided that he would have to be bound out too. He was placed under the guardianship of the owner of the same livery stable where he had worked. He works hard there grooming horses in the mornings, but all he gets in return is a place to stay and a little food. He's always hungry like me, and he often has time on his hands. No one pays attention or cares about him."

Tagger was saddened by these stories. Why had life been so cruel to these poor orphan children?

After she and Renaud delivered the catch at Gina's, she watched as he headed off to the blacksmith's to fry his fish. What a good person he seemed to be; he deserved so much more out of life.

With the help of Diane and the boys, Tagger's business started picking up immediately. The sale of the larger catches enabled her to buy pound nets for catching shore fish, and an old cart she bought from a fisherman to carry the fish to Gina's. Mary taught her how to catch the shore fish with the nets.

Little by little, Tagger's young employees became more skilled at fishing, and as soon as they could leave their situations, usually about noon, they ran to the pier. They too knew that winter was coming and they'd have to save some of their fish to eat during the cold months ahead. The more they saved, the more they needed to catch, so soon they were all staying at the pier until well past sunset.

Tagger knew the others needed more than just fish to help them through the winter, so she decided to give them a choice. She told them they could either keep half their catch or sell it to her for money. This way, with their earned money, they could buy the other supplies they too needed, such as clothes and soap and cornmeal.

Sometimes they took the cash, but most of the time, they kept their share of the catch. Food was still the most important staple to them. Mary also taught them all how to salt and dry their fish, so they'd last longer.

Two more weeks passed. Because of the importance of bread in their diet, Tagger arranged with Betty at the lodging house for all of them to work there on Saturdays. They worked as a team to clean the whole downstairs and the guest rooms. In return, each received a week's supply of bread. They enjoyed the camaraderie of working together, and Betty made sure they received a bonus of vegetables and fruits when they were available from the sailing expeditions in from Florida and the Caribbean.

Soon Betty, Gina and the children had gotten close enough to Tagger to realize there was no father with ague or any other disease. They understood how important it was for her to make it on her own and were only too happy to help her guard the secret. But her fear became theirs too. How in the world would the town allow a little boy to live alone?

CHAPTER 16
The Lessons

A cool breeze inbound from the ocean blew across the chimney like the gasp of a ghost. It was still late summer, but the wind hinted of the fall and the winter that would follow it.

Now that they had become friends, Tagger agreed to let Gina teach her a few basics of arithmetic and reading. She didn't want to impose on Gina, but with her little business growing so fast, she barely had enough knowledge to manage it.

"You'd be such an energetic student if you could go to school," Gina said, "and you learn so quickly."

"It's important for me to make it on my own," Tagger replied. "You'll teach me everything I need to know."

They began with the letters of the alphabet and soon the words quickly came for Tagger.

One day, Tagger said, "I can read a few words now, but I still want you to read to me."

Gina smiled. "All right, but I'll let you practice on the easy parts."

They spent many long evenings in Gina's comfortable living room reading parts of her many books. Tagger learned about morality and the spirit of mankind from Alexander Pope's *Essay on Man*. She discovered the complexities of the weather from *The Farmer's Almanac*, and when Gina read some of *Common Sense*, she was absolutely thrilled to find out that Thomas Paine felt the same way about freedom that she did. He had written that the American colonies, now new states, were founded on a desire for freedom. Freedom was Tagger's most sacred desire too.

When they finished reading parts of each of the books, the two of them would discuss what it meant to them. Gina loved this as much as Tagger, because she could see that Tagger was so receptive to new ideas.

Tagger liked *Aesop's Fables* the best. The animal characters weren't always good or lovable, but they were uncomplicated and believable—like people she knew.

Her favorite fable was the story of the thirsty raven. The raven needed a drink—badly. He spotted some cool, clear water in a tall vase with a long, narrow neck. But he couldn't drink from the vase, because he would get his head stuck.

He thought of knocking the pitcher over. But that meant he could only hope for one or two drinks before the water ran off and sank into the earth.

Instead, the resourceful raven figured out that if he filled the vase with pebbles, one by one, the level of the water would rise until he could drink easily. It took him a long time to fill the vase with the small stones, but the water was even more satisfying, because he'd worked so hard to get it.

"The poor raven," said Gina, when Tagger read the story aloud all by herself. "He went through so much for just a drink."

"No Gina, you shouldn't feel sorry for him. He earned his own reward. No one helped him. He used his brain to solve his problem, and it made him proud. The water meant so much more to him that way, and it lasted longer."

Gina looked at the little boy, and marveled at the child's youthful wisdom. "Of course you're right, Tagger, but it takes a strong person to wait for the reward."

"Yes, it does, Gina," Tagger replied with a confidence far beyond her years. "But save your pity for the raven, Gina. I think we should only pity people who won't use the talents they have to help themselves. Not everyone is smart or strong or beautiful, but everyone has at least one good quality they can rely on.

"You know who I pity," Tagger continued, "the owners of the other butcher shops in town. They never try to have better meat and fish. All they do is to try to make your business fail."

"Yes. Yes, you're right. Now, wait a minute, who's teaching who here?" Gina wagged her finger at Tagger. They both laughed.

As their laughter turned to giggles, Tagger thought how much Gina reminded her of the fable characters. She always remained so constant and stable, even under adversity. She was friendly and understanding. She had an inner strength that she couldn't see for herself, but Tagger could see it in her so clearly.

It became important for Tagger to help Gina regain her confidence. They both needed it. Tagger dreamed of increasing her fishing business, of catching more and finer fish. While many people along the Mystic River caught their own fish, there was a large market among those who didn't go out in boats, such as the farmers, the shop keepers and the elderly. Tagger just wanted them to have the best fish at the lowest prices.

She needed for Gina's business to grow and expand, not just for her sake and the other children's, but for Gina's sake as well.

When Gina bustled around the spotless kitchen, preparing hot tea or cookies for her little student, Tagger would watch her and wonder if her own mother had ever been like this. Had she ever been sensitive and giving, like the older lady? If so, why had she deserted her? Did she have a choice? Was she still alive? Sometimes, she just had to make herself quit thinking about the past, because it could eat her up inside.

Gina was always sorry when Tagger left at the end of a pleasant evening. She hated to see her go out into the darkness, but Tagger didn't really mind the walk back to her cottage.

The evening breeze was cool and invigorating, and it always made her think about how happy she was to be free. As free as the wind. The village was peaceful during this hour of the evening.

Tonight, all was quiet. It had been just three months since she had come to the area, but she had come to know it well. Some of the shops along Main Street in Portersville were still open, but the owners were either cleaning up or casting impatient glances at lingering customers. In the mercantile, Mr. Markle had already turned off a couple of lamps in hopes of speeding up his dawdling customer, but it hadn't worked. The slender, gray-haired lady who was sorting through cooking utensils took no notice.

Tagger followed the gravel street past the neat little houses that made up the residential section of Portersville. Most of the houses were very similar, except for the color of the wooden walls and shutters. The little bungalows looked so inviting. Smoke curled from the chimneys, and the warm glow of lamps and candles filled the dark street.

Tagger knew only a little about love, but she was certain the hard-working families behind the doors of those homes understood it. She felt a twinge of loneliness at the thought.

The comely village women, including Mrs. Anderson, would be finishing the last of the dinner dishes or rocking in front of the fireplace with their mending. The fathers of the village would be reading or maybe whittling, and their stern voices would tolerate no back talk when they ordered the little ones to bed. And Betty at the lodging house would be sitting and talking with her husband in the late hours of the evening. A relaxed calm had spread over Portersville.

The lights from the village began to fade away as Tagger headed south from town. Gina had loaned her a lantern, but it was so dark tonight she had to walk carefully to be sure she stayed on the path. She knew the bends and turns well, so she could keep up a fairly steady pace.

Suddenly an unfamiliar light shone up ahead. It was coming from the schoolhouse. The students had been gone for hours, and she'd never known the schoolmaster to stay so late. Her curiosity got the best of her. She set down the lantern several yards back from the school house and then she crept up to the rough, wooden windowsill to peek inside.

There sat the schoolmaster, serious as ever. He was working on something at his desk at the front of the room. Tagger ducked down because she was facing him directly. She was afraid he'd look up and see her spying at him. Ever so slowly, she raised up enough to peer back into the room.

He was holding something in his lap, between his knees. He was hitting it with a hammer, pounding nails, it appeared.

Tagger watched this mysterious behavior for a few moments and then saw the schoolmaster set a small, brown leather shoe on the desk. He inspected it thoroughly, stern in his appraisal. After he was satisfied with its appearance, he bent down and picked up something else, probably the other shoe, and started the whole process over again.

Several nails later, he set the second shoe beside the first, scrutinizing them both with the same cold look he'd used on her the first day of school. Then slowly, his drawn face broke into a radiant smile.

Rising from his high-backed wood and leather chair, he picked up the pair of shoes and almost tiptoed over the polished wooden floor to the third student desk in the first row by the blackboard. He lifted the desktop and gently set the shoes inside.

Tagger didn't know what to make of this, but she was sure it indicated some act of kindness. His smile gave him away.

She was confused. She'd believed the mean schoolmaster was her foe. She had vowed to show him up, prove him wrong. Now she had caught him doing something good.

Tagger struggled with the scene she had just witnessed as she picked up the lantern and trudged back to her cottage; she was becoming very tired. While she was getting ready for bed, she realized that maybe she'd been wrong to hate the schoolmaster. She wished she knew him better. Maybe he was actually a good man.

Perhaps someday she would get the chance to learn from him as Gina had suggested. But how?

CHAPTER 17
The Sale

The days became shorter, but more productive. The winter flounder were coming into shore, but the summer flounder hadn't left yet, so the catches were large. The Fish Children, as the town had begun to call them, worked hard. They were storing fish and saving money as well for winter. Tagger noticed that Edward badly needed new clothes that would fit his long arms and legs.

At the end of an excellent day of fishing, when the sun had begun to sink into the western sky, Tagger paid the Fish Children, the boys with fish and Diane with money. They packed their gear and headed off to prepare their suppers. She knew they also had a good supply of bread and cheese they'd earned at the lodging house, so she wasn't worried about them tonight.

After the others were gone, Tagger saw that she was left with the biggest catch ever. She filled her cart with the catch, and it groaned from the weight of eight, fresh fish.

When he saw Tagger with the heavy load, Renaud ran up quickly and grabbed the iron handle of the cart. "Here, let me help. That's too heavy for you."

"No, Renaud," she insisted. "I can handle it, and I know you're hungry. Go home and eat."

Reluctantly, he let her go. He knew by now that when Tagger was determined to do something, nothing could stop this boy.

Laboriously Tagger pulled the cart to town, but she didn't really mind the heavy load. Another problem tugged at the back of her mind though.

Would Gina be able to sell her catch? If not, what would they do? None of the other butchers wanted to deal with her. She was concerned but not really worried yet. Something would work out; at least Gina would buy most of the catch and . . .

But as she turned the corner into the town square, Tagger couldn't believe her eyes. Several customers were crowded into Gina's store, and a line had formed outside. What could have happened? As she neared, she quickly saw the reason.

Gina was having a sale. Although the townspeople were still a little skeptical of her meat and seafood, they just couldn't resist the low prices. The windows of the small shop were covered with yellow banners with red writing, proclaiming the sale and the sale prices.

Gina was flushed and happy as she hurried about waiting on the rush of customers. Tagger went to the back door and called in. Gina excused herself from a woman buying five pounds of pork and slipped into the back room to greet her friend.

"Tagger, I'm so glad you're here," she smiled excitedly. "I'm about to run out of fish. Look at that catch you have! I'll take all of them, and I'll give you two and a half cents for each."

"This is wonderful, Gina. The sale is a stroke of genius." Gina hurried to the register to get Tagger's payment. When she returned, Tagger was already loading the fish into the ice chest where Gina kept her reserves. They could hear the deliveryman from the slaughterhouse waiting outside to bring in the fresh meat Gina had ordered from them. Gina returned to serve the group of customers waiting at the counter.

Because of her good fortune with the fish sale, Tagger decided she would give her Fish Children each a bonus of one penny per fish they caught. They were good young people, proud, hard working, and they liked taking responsibility for themselves.

You could see the glee in Edward's face the time he'd pulled in a huge sea bass; everyone clapped in delight. He pretended he didn't care about the attention he was getting, but he was clearly overjoyed.

Diane had pulled out of her shell and even began to play little innocent pranks and joke around with the others. Soon she became the one to keep everyone else going when the fishing was slow or the weather made the day seem long and friendless. And of course, Renaud was true and faithful to Tagger whenever she needed him. He was always willing to lend her a hand with her work and supported her when she had new ideas.

The best part was that the guardians of these orphans let them work each afternoon. Or was it that they didn't care if the children lived or died as long as the work was done?

Diane was Tagger's closest friend. When Tagger fought the loneliness and the shadows of the past, Diane would assure her the pain would ease with time, that someday she'd have a family of her own. This all seemed unlikely to Tagger, since she was still assuming the safe role of a boy. Diane often looked at her with wondering eyes. Did she suspect Tagger was a girl? Tagger was still trying hard to keep up the ruse—cutting her hair every week with the expensive scissors she'd managed to buy weeks ago. Even if she did suspect, Diane said nothing.

Whenever Tagger felt good and wanted to share her future plans, Diane would listen seriously, her green eyes shining in her round face. She too had dreams to add to the conversation.

Diane wanted a little beach cottage by the ocean, someday. When spring came, she'd open the shutters and the windows and let the warm sea breeze fill the house. She planned to have a loving husband and several children scampering about, playing on the beach. Maybe they'd even have a dog, a big red one like she'd seen next to Gina's market.

The fishing was outstanding over the next few afternoons. The Fish Children were happy, some for the first time since they'd lost their parents. They began looking up to Tagger as a fair-minded brother instead of an employer. But the important thing was that they worked as a team and helped each other.

Gina redoubled her efforts to improve her business. She told her steady customers she would give them reduced prices if they'd tell their friends about her shop. She even ran advertisements in the tiny village paper. Soon word of the fine meat and fish buys spread to the nearby villages of Mystic Bridge, Stonington and Groton. Gina's business boomed.

One day Mary began to teach Tagger how to tong for oysters in the shallow water of the sound from the small open rowboat she had. In a way Tagger was Mary's eyes as the old woman's eyesight seemed to get worse week by week.

Oysters could mean a significant change to her business. Because they were caught in the months with "r's"— September, October, November, December, January, February, March, and April, the oyster catches would provide her with income during the winter months as well.

Just when things seemed to be going so well, Tagger grew careless. It was a warm evening in early September. Tagger was doing her "laundry" in the stream. She wanted to wash everything, so she'd put on the old dress she still had from her life at Miss Devlin's. She was bent over the stream, scrubbing clothes, when she heard the sound.

Someone or something was thrashing about in the woods! No one ever came this way. She guessed it was fear of the haunted cottage or because her location was far away from the normal path people took to Noank. At any rate, the sound took her by surprise.

She jumped up from the stream just as the hunter burst through the woods into the clearing. It surprised both of them when they ran into each other. Tagger screamed in alarm.

The hunter, Tagger realized immediately, was William Cooper. Gina had told her he was from Noank and traded furs in Groton. He stopped dead, dropped his gun to his side, and gawked at the dress. And then he slowly began to realize the situation. "Why you're Tagger. I, er we or well, everyone thought you were a boy. Why, you're a girl! Where's your pa?" he said, looking into the cottage. It didn't take long for the truth to dawn on him.

"There is no pa, is there? You're a young girl, living alone," he said accusingly.

Tagger was frightened. She didn't answer, fearful he might mistreat her in some way.

"Well, we'll have to see about this. We can't have any girls living alone here. It's not seemly. You need a guardian—someone to take responsibility for you, someone to raise you like a lady. I'll have to notify the sheriff."

"No, please," Tagger pleaded, "Don't tell the sheriff. I don't need a guardian. I'm fine here on my own."

The hunter didn't argue with her—this mere girl; he knew he was right. He just looked at her and continued on through the woods, shaking his head. Tagger shuddered as she watched him go. She supposed she knew this would have to happen. But what would become of her now?

CHAPTER 18
The Sheriff

The next morning, while Tagger was waiting for a brief rainstorm to pass over, she sat on the floor of the cottage, sorting hooks and lines. Suddenly she heard a loud knocking on the door. She jumped to her feet quickly.

When she opened the old, warped door just a crack, she saw a large man dressed in business clothes. It was Sheriff Anderson with his wife Priscilla. In a booming voice, he bellowed, "Let me in; I need to talk to you."

"Yes, sir," she replied dejectedly, opening the door all the way. She'd been expecting him.

The sheriff and his wife stepped into the old cottage; his large presence seemed overwhelming in the small space. He took a long time surveying the interior, as he studied her living conditions. He seemed surprised that Tagger had made the cottage so livable. Old wooden boxes served as chairs and tables. A small beat-up bed frame held her blanket.

"I understand your name is Tagger. Is that true?" he asked.

"Yes, my name is Tagger."

"Bill Cooper, down Noank way, told me a girl is living here alone. Is that right?"

Tagger had dressed in her boy's clothes again, hoping that Mr. Cooper wouldn't turn her in, so she knew the sheriff was confused. But there was no point in trying to continue the charade. "Yes sir, I'm a girl," she said pulling off the old felt hat that she'd worn everywhere for weeks now.

"Anyone else live here with you?" he asked, staring at her.

"No," she replied miserably.

Mrs. Anderson saw how dejected and afraid Tagger was and prodded the sheriff in the side with her elbow. But he too had begun to feel sorry for Tagger and her impossible situation and lightened his tone. "You know my friend Richard Owen used to live here. He was a bachelor—never fixed this place up much. But he was a good man. A lot of folks resented him because he was trying to make something of himself, but all he wanted was to provide his customers with the best products from his mill. His death was a sad thing. Just a freak accident in a storm. Guess you picked a good place to hide out. Most everyone thinks this place is haunted."

"I didn't know him," Tagger replied, trying to hold her head up, "but I heard how he died. I just needed a place to live and nobody bothered me here."

"Well, the truth is the town of Groton owns this property. Owen didn't have close kin. An uncle came and cleared out his belongings, but there were back taxes on the place, so he just left it sit. The town took it under warranty. I see you have no furniture. You need a proper bed. We can't have you living like this!"

"Where are you from, dear?" Mrs. Anderson asked gently. "Where are your parents?"

Tagger was truly frightened now. She didn't want Mrs. Anderson and the sheriff to know she'd run away from Miss Devlin's. "I was separated from my parents when I was younger. I was kept in servitude by a lady who made me work very hard. She wouldn't let me go to school or have friends, so I ran away. She never had any papers on me."

The Andersons nodded as they listened. The sheriff would have to think about this. "Tagger, there are laws in the state of Connecticut about the maintenance of orphan children. It's the responsibility of this town to find you a guardian."

When Tagger seemed confused by the term "guardian," he went on to explain, "Each child in this state must have an adult who is responsible for his or her upbringing—someone who will sign papers saying they are responsible. Usually that means we have to find a family who will take care of you and make sure you're raised properly."

Tagger was shaken by his words. She didn't want to live with anyone unless it was her own family. She couldn't let herself be a drain on a family in the village. Her pride just wouldn't allow her to accept that.

The sheriff read the concern in Tagger's face. He looked at her compassionately and wondered at the fact she had lived so long and so successfully by herself. "I have no choice but to bring this situation up with the town selectmen at our next meeting. The selectmen will have to decide what's in your best interest."

Tagger had no choice but to agree. She nodded.

"You need to tell me who held you in servitude. If you say you were held without papers, you will become a ward of the town."

"Miss Rita Devlin," she whispered reluctantly, barely able to speak her name. "She owned the Light Horse Inn in Groton."

Sheriff Anderson exchanged glances with his wife. "This

is Wednesday, Tagger," he said. "I'm going to call an emergency meeting of the town selectmen for tomorrow night. You can stay here until I come back Friday with their decision."

Mrs. Anderson bent down and patted Tagger on the shoulder. "Goodbye for now, dear. Take care of yourself and don't be frightened. This will all work out."

She watched silently as the Andersons left the way they'd come, carefully skirting the mud puddles in the path as they went. What would she do?

Tagger worried all day and into the night about the sheriff's visit. She tossed and turned, fighting the blanket, wondering the outcome of the selectmen meeting, knowing how much it could change her life.

If she were placed with a family in the village, would they let her go to school? Or would she be destined to clean and scrub for years like she'd done at Miss Devlin's?

Before she drifted off to a tortured sleep, she thought of Gina. She needed to talk to her. Perhaps she could offer some suggestions. Gina knew how important it was to her to maintain her independence.

The look on Gina's face was one of sheer confusion when Tagger went to her shop, bright and early the next morning in her dress.

"Tagger, you're a girl?" she said dumbly.

"Yes, Gina. I'm sorry I deceived you and the others in town, but I had no choice. I knew I would never be allowed to live alone if the town knew I was a girl. You know how important it is for me to be on my own?"

"Well, yes of course, dear, but—well you certainly fooled me." Gina stared at her in disbelief. "But what made you decide to drop the disguise?"

Tagger told her about the hunter, the visit from the sheriff and his wife and the meeting of the assembly.

"Why yes," Gina said, "I saw the announcement about the meeting posted in town today. I would have never guessed that it involved you. Oh Tagger, what has happened to you in the past that would cause you to go to these extremes to hide your identity?"

Slowly, and with difficulty, Tagger told Gina everything. "So you see," she concluded, "I believe my mother sold me into servitude. That's the last I remember."

Gina's heart went out to this brave little girl. She was so young, yet she had managed to take care of herself, start her own business and begin an education—all on her own.

The terrible story of her life had brought tears to both their eyes, and Gina comforted her in her large bosom, trying to think of something encouraging to say.

"Let's wait to see how the meeting turns out," she offered. "I may have an idea or two. I know the town is just acting in your best interest. Let's wait until Friday to see what they've decided."

CHAPTER 19
Friday

True to his word, Sheriff Anderson arrived at Tagger's cottage at eight o'clock Friday morning, the day after the meeting of the selectmen. When Tagger opened the door, she saw that he was accompanied by another tall man wearing the business garb of the day: long, black woolen cut away coat and trousers, gray vest, and a white shirt with a rounded collar.

Sheriff Anderson introduced the white-haired gentleman as James Sherman. "He's the selectman in Groton," the sheriff explained. "Portersville is a district of Groton. Mr. Sherman represents the area where you live."

Mr. Sherman patted Tagger's hand gently, then he looked around the cottage. He too was amazed that such a young girl could have made this old place so livable.

"Now, Tagger, I'm not here to frighten you, but it's my duty to tell you the outcome of the meeting last night. First of all, everyone admires your courage in trying to live alone here, but you can't stay here. The cottage belongs to the town of Groton. Since there was no one to pay taxes on the place after the former resident died, we had to take it over."

"How much are the taxes?" Tagger asked timidly.

"Oh now, child, they're much too high for you to consider. Why, they're ten dollars a year," he exclaimed, certain that this would seem like a huge number to a little girl.

"And," he continued, "the second thing is that you're a minor and you can't be allowed to live on your own. You must have a guardian—someone to raise you. Someone to take legal responsibility for you. There are quite simply state laws which must be followed, and they are for your own good. You must have good food to eat, clothing and a warm shelter. And you must be taken to church and taught to read."

With the exception of the church, she already had everything he'd mentioned. Considering the awful, fiery diatribe she'd heard a minister deliver to his congregation one day as she passed the church, she doubted she had missed much in that regard either.

"So," Mr. Sherman continued, "what the Groton selectmen have decreed is that Sheriff Anderson must find you a guardian and a place for you live by the end of next week."

Tagger was silent. She considered telling Mr. Sherman that she was self-sufficient now. She had a business, employees, salted fish and vegetables to get her through the winter and a little money to fix up the cottage. But she knew it would be to no avail. She was no match for these "official" men from the village.

"Now, we want to make this as easy for you as we can," Mr. Sherman soothed clumsily. "The selectmen admire you for your strength in this ordeal. Sheriff Anderson recognized the name of your former mistress from the inn in Groton. We went to investigate. Shameful! She wouldn't tell us the name of your mother, either, although we believe that when she sold you into servitude, she left the country."

"The district of Portersville is your home now," Mr. Sherman consoled her, "and we will be your parents in absentia. But as an independent village, we don't want to

destroy your spirit in the process. If there's someone you know who would let you move in and become your guardian, you just tell the sheriff here. We'll try to do what's best for you."

Tagger nodded, totally at a loss for words. How could she convey to him that she did not want to live with someone else—with strangers who might stand in the way of her plans?

The two men turned to go, but as they headed down the path, the sheriff turned and said as gently as possible, "I'm sorry, Tagger, but you have only one week here, no more. I'll be back with the guardianship papers then. The town wants to solve its orphan problem in a fair and understanding manner, and it's my duty to carry out their decision."

The sheriff's words rang in her ears as she walked to the pier later that day, "you have one week here, no more." Shocked faces greeted her. Renaud and Edward were speechless. Diane, having all along suspected that Tagger was a girl, only wondered why she had suddenly forgone her disguise.

Tagger didn't need them to prod her for answers. She knew she had to tell them everything, and quickly. Their futures were at stake too. If she were placed in a home, the fishing business could be in jeopardy.

After the reality of the situation set in with the boys, and they finally saw that Tagger was a girl now and a pretty one at that, they offered their support. But Diane was the one to offer the first practical suggestion.

"I think Gina might be the answer, Tagger. The sheriff said someone has to sign papers to be your guardian. Gina would do that. Maybe you could still live on your own some way. What do you boys think?"

"I know the orphan rules are strict here, especially for girls," Renaud stated. And then glumly he continued, "We could vouch for her, but we're just viewed as misfits here too."

"Wish her well, Renaud," Diane admonished. "Tagger needs us to cheer her up, so she can face whatever is ahead for her."

Tagger took Diane's advice and set off for Gina's. She smiled back at the Fish Children confidently despite the fact that she was apprehensive. Was this too much to ask Gina? And how could the sheriff and the selectmen even consider her proposal to live by herself?

Gina wasn't surprised to see Tagger today; she'd heard the results of the selectmen's meeting. She welcomed her in cheerfully and began to scurry around making tea and biscuits. When they were seated in Gina's cozy living room, sipping and munching, Tagger explained why she was there.

"Gina, the sheriff says I must have a guardian, someone to take legal responsibility for me. You know I'm quite able to take care of myself now, now that you're selling our fish. I was hoping, well, I was wondering, if you would be my guardian. I wouldn't cause you any trouble, I promise."

"Oh Tagger, you know how much I love you and the other children," Gina replied sincerely. "Of course, I'll be your guardian. But I want you to come here and live with me. I have a shed in the back. We can get some builders to add an addition, get you some furniture, and I could cook for you. It wouldn't be any trouble at all."

Tagger was dumbstruck. "Gina, I can't let you do that. I'm fine with the life I have. I have a place to stay; it's not much, but it's home to me. And now I have bread and plenty of fish to eat. I get by quite well. I just need an official legal guardian."

They discussed the guardianship for some time, until Gina finally gave in. This was truly a courageous child. It was terribly important for her to prove herself and to have her freedom. Gina hated to concede, but she knew Tagger would never be happy taking charity from anyone.

The next day, Gina and Tagger walked to a two-story wooden house near the village square. The sheriff's office was on the first floor. He and Mrs. Anderson lived upstairs.

Sheriff Anderson rose when they came in and greeted them heartily. "Sit down," he said pointing to two chairs opposite his desk. He was aware of some of the rumors that had gone around about Gina, but he was a reasonable man. He knew they were merely the inventions of jealous competitors.

After Gina explained the plan for her to be Tagger's guardian while she continued to live on her own, he was surprised and definitely skeptical. "Gina," he said. "You know Tagger needs a family. She can't live by herself."

"Yes, I agree," Gina said. "But you don't know this young lady. She's strong and responsible. I'll be glad to take full responsibility for her and make sure she's well and safe. You know I mix herbal medicines, and I can provide the remedies and receipts she needs if she's ill. I see her all the time at the shop, and I promise to visit her home at least twice a week. If she can't make it on her own, I'll be the first to recommend you find her a home. But I'll tell you right now, it won't be necessary."

The sheriff stared at Gina for a while, unsure what to say next. Slowly, he leaned back in his chair and folded his arms across his chest. "Gina, perhaps you could be her employer. We could arrange for her to be bound out to you. I think the selectmen would accept that."

"In a way, she already works for me," Gina explained. "She's my fish supplier. Tagger has started a fishing business and has just hired three other orphans. They are a bit older than she and work for her in their spare time. The Fish Children provide me with all the fish they don't eat, and I pay them one-half cent per pound. It's actually working quite well. With her extra money, Tagger has been able to improve her cottage and buy herself items that she can't catch or grow, like soap and corn meal.

"Also, Tagger has invented a little pouch that she calls the 'tagger pouch.' Mr. Markle buys them from her and sells them to his customers. I help her make these, and we both receive a few extra pennies to help us get by. She is truly an inventive and remarkable girl," Gina concluded.

After some consideration, Sheriff Anderson said, "All right, Gina, this is what we'll do. I'll make a report to the selectmen requesting that you be her guardian and that Tagger be allowed to stay where she is. If they agree, you will sign the guardianship papers, and then each month, you will sign a report saying that you vouch for her well-being and that you have seen her four times each week. Do you agree?"

"Yes, I do," Gina nodded solemnly.

As they were leaving, Sheriff Anderson called out, "Wait a minute. I forgot one important matter. The taxes on the cottage. If Tagger is to stay there, someone must pay the taxes."

Before Gina could answer, Tagger said simply, "I will pay them."

"And I'll stand surety for her," Gina added without hesitation.

By now, both Sheriff Anderson and Gina knew Tagger

would do just that, so all he could say was, "I'll pass that on to the selectmen as well. They're meeting Thursday night. I'll let you know their decision on Friday. And," he rose to walk with them to the door, "I'll see that a large supply of firewood, a mattress, and a table is sent to you, Tagger."

"Yes," said Mrs. Anderson, "and have the delivery men build a little privacy shed. A lady shouldn't have to go to the woods."

As promised, Sheriff Anderson arrived at Gina's butcher shop on Friday morning. After he and Gina had exchanged pleasantries, Sheriff Anderson handed Gina the guardianship papers for Tagger. "The selectmen have agreed to let Tagger live alone as long as you promise to keep careful watch over her, report on her monthly, and introduce her to a church. The schoolmaster will see that she receives her schooling. We're a progressive village here and realize the importance of education. Also, Mr. Sherman even agreed to reduce the annual tax fee on Tagger's house."

He went on to say, "As you know, Gina, New England has many orphans now. There's so much disease and changing conditions. But we think this is a unique situation, and since the town of Groton and the district of Portersville is proud of its independent tradition."

Gina nodded her thanks.

Sheriff Anderson walked out of the shop with a smile on his face, seemingly pleased with himself for resolving yet another problem in his community.

CHAPTER 20
Church and School

The decision of the selectmen pleased Gina, Tagger and the Fish Children. The fishing business was intact, and Tagger was able to continue to make her tagger pouches without interruption. It was all perfect, except for one problem. Tagger was loath to go to church. Church attendance was a condition of her independence, but she dreaded the requirement to comply.

Her cottage was located in close proximity to the Mariners Church located just outside of Portersville. Church attendance had been required during colonial days in New England, with a fine levied for nonattendance. The Mariners Church was built in 1825 to house the Methodist, Congregationalist and Baptist religions and to facilitate attendance in the Mystic River area.

Therefore, Tagger had her choice. All she had to do was attend one of these denominational services. But her experience with the church was not positive.

Sunday after Sunday, she saw parents drag their protesting children to the church. Sometimes the sermons were calm, but sometimes a minister of one of the denominations would scream his warnings of a fearsome God who saw to it that disbelievers burned in agony in the depths of Hell. She shuddered whenever she thought about attending, even though she knew Gina would be with her.

Gina approached Sheriff Anderson about the dilemma one day. "Must I make her attend? The poor child is terrified, and she works so hard all week. It seems a shame to force her to attend church against her will."

"Yes, Gina, I'm sorry. You know it's a requirement." He thought a moment. "You know, I have an idea. There's a church in New Haven that's starting up that may interest Tagger. It's called the Unitarian Church—Unitarian because they believe in the unity of God as opposed to the idea of the Trinity or God in three persons. Now this probably isn't important to Tagger, who has little knowledge of orthodox religions anyway, but the Unitarian church is known for its more liberal view of religion. They're more accepting of independent religious thinking. Perhaps that notion will be easier for her to accept."

"But New Haven is too far away for her," Gina replied.

"Yes, of course it is, but the Mariners Church has invited the minister of that church as a guest speaker this Sunday. His name is Reverend Elmore Sturbridge, and I understand that a local man from Portersville, Harold Evings, has been studying the religion as well in hopes of starting a church here someday soon. He will be attending this week too. Why don't you give it a try."

"All right, perhaps I can convince Tagger," Gina offered.

Tagger liked the idea of independent religious thinking and agreed to give it a try. Sunday morning came, and Tagger dressed to attend church. Gina had made her a simple blue dress with a long skirt and an empire waistline. Everyone who saw her dressed like this was shocked. Her curly hair was beginning to grow out too, and they saw what a lovely girl she had turned out to be.

She and Gina sat very near the back of the church in case

Tagger wanted to make a quick exit, but as the service continued, they both found the soft-spoken Reverend Sturbridge interesting, even comforting. He spoke of tolerance and acceptance of differing views, and he compared the important aspects of various religions. The congregation gasped when he mentioned that former President Thomas Jefferson had believed in the concept of Unitarianism.

Afterwards, she and Gina met the minister. It wasn't difficult; few attendees had chosen to meet him. Most of the townspeople left the church shaking their heads at his unusual views.

While they talked with Reverend Sturbridge, Harold Evings came up and introduced himself. He too was mild-mannered. He explained that the Mariners Church had agreed to give him a small meeting room in the basement to discuss Unitarian philosophies in the future. The Reverend Sturbridge wished him well and asked Gina and Tagger if they would attend.

The issue of religion had been resolved. This was the beginning of Gina and Tagger's weekly pursuit of an alternative religion that would grow in the area over the years to come. One by one the other orphans joined them in the damp basement of the church where they would freely discuss their religious views and ethical beliefs without fear of censure. Betty, who now owned the lodging house, became a regular attendee too, and Sheriff Anderson was even known to come on a few occasions.

When autumn leaves began to turn and fall from the trees, Tagger's excitement grew. She knew she would be going to the late fall session of school soon. Gina had continued to teach her to read; every night they worked, often far into the night. How fast she was learning, Gina marvelled. Words flew as Tagger read page after page. "Your gifts are many," Gina whispered.

Still, Tagger was far behind; most of the children her age would be several years ahead of her. But this didn't stop her, she longed to know about the secrets the distinguished teacher would share this year at the old red schoolhouse.

How would she enroll? Would Gina take her? Would the others students reject her, make fun of her, ostracize her because she was an orphan?

How would she deal with the stern schoolmaster?

The question of Tagger's education answered itself one Friday night soon after Gina had signed the guardianship papers. Tagger was alone on the pier. It happened eerily, and the events to follow would change her life.

The lowering sun cast pearly shadows across the sky as she packed up her equipment and prepared for her late afternoon trip to Gina's market. The others had left a few minutes earlier, going their separate directions.

It had been a good day. She was putting the last bluefish into the cart, when she heard an adult voice. It came from the long, swaying shadows near the shoreline.

"Your business is doing quite well, young lady," said the voice. It was a man's voice, low, but authoritative. She recognized the sound of his voice, but couldn't remember where she'd heard it. This was the first time since she'd been coming to the pier that she'd seen a grownup here.

"Who's there," she called out.

"Mr. Jensen," the man replied as he stepped onto the pier and into the fading sunlight.

Tagger could barely make out his features. She looked

carefully and to her surprise, saw it was the schoolmaster—
the strange man with the thin lips and penetrating eyes, the
same man who had stopped her from going to school so long
ago. He stared at her intently as he came nearer.

Tagger was somewhat frightened, but she held her ground.
This was her territory; she was in control here. She wouldn't
let him intimidate her this time.

"You've done very well for yourself," he said firmly, but with
no malice.

"Yes, I've had good help from the Fish Children; we work
well together. Why have you come here?" Tagger asked,
trying to sound as calm and as mature as possible.

"I came to see when you're going to get some formal
schooling." He was smiling now, almost impishly. "It's about
time, you know."

Tagger was flabbergasted. "But, but you wouldn't . . ."

"Wouldn't let you come into the schoolhouse," he finished
for her. "You're right, but you weren't ready then. I didn't
realize that you had no parents nor anyone to enroll you and
pay the fees. But you still weren't ready to take the sneers
and jokes from the other children. You were so shy; you had
no strength to face that kind of cruel rejection. Your only need
then was to survive."

Tagger paused and stared at Mr. Jensen; she was too excited
to respond. And then finally, "I suppose you're right, but I
am ready to learn now."

"Yes, that you are; but now I'm afraid we've almost waited
too long, and you're too busy. I understand you plan to bring
in oysters in the winter months as well."

"Yes, that's true," she agreed regretfully. "It will be difficult
to attend school during the day."

Mr. Jensen grinned again. It was a simple, genuine but mirthful smile. It was the same smile he'd had the night she'd spied at him through the window at the schoolhouse, the night he was fixing the shoes. "But how about in the evenings?"

"Evenings?" she said, "What a generous offer. I'm already taking lessons. I can read pretty well," she went on proudly. "And I can divide 16,838 by 563."

He was fairly beaming now, and Tagger wanted to hug him, but thought better of it. She must be more reserved until she was sure he could be trusted.

"Come to the schoolhouse at six o'clock tomorrow night," he instructed, "and we shall begin."

"Oh thank you sir; you've made me very happy. I'll work so hard."

"I have no doubt of that," Mr. Jensen said sincerely, as he turned to leave the pier. But then he stopped suddenly and spun back around. He had one more surprise for Tagger.

Digging into the big pocket of his loose-fitting brown overcoat, he pulled out a well-worn, leather-bound book with a title stamped in gold. There was just enough light remaining for Tagger to read the title: *Piscatorial Encounters—A Guide for the Expert Fisherman.*

"I almost forgot your first assignment. Read chapters one and two for discussion in class," Mr. Jensen ordered with pretended sternness.

CHAPTER 21
The Education

When she arrived back at her cottage late that evening, she could hardly wait to start the book Mr. Jensen had given her. The usual routine of her evening had to come first though, and it seemed to take forever, but in reality she cooked supper and cleaned up with record speed. She lit a fire in the fireplace. The sheriff's wood burned well. Finally she was ready to curl up near a bright, whale-oil lamp on the new mattress the town had provided. She opened the treasured book, *A Guide for the Expert Fisherman*!

She read fast and with great interest. A new world was opening for her.

She learned that fish had family and species names, and that there were countless ways they could be caught and landed. There was page after page of various types of hooks, lines, poles, reels, nets, dredges and baits, with beautiful drawings to show the examples.

As she read on and on, she discovered that weather conditions, migration habits and even tides affected the feeding patterns of fish. This was useful information, indeed, to a fisherman.

All of this knowledge gave her a heady feeling of excitement. It was only after she finished the last glorious page that she realized she'd read late into the night.

The next day, she learned that Mr. Jensen had a fine education himself. He was born in England and had studied at Cambridge and then for a year at the Sorbonne in France. But during all his years of schooling, he said he had never seen a student as thrilled with the pursuit of knowledge as Tagger. She fairly bubbled that first night of class.

When they began to discuss the first chapters of *Piscatorial Encounters*, Mr. Jensen soon realized she'd read the entire book. Even more astounding was the fact that she understood it well enough to explain it to him.

"You were up all night reading, weren't you, Tagger?" Mr. Jensen asked in astonishment.

"Yes, this was just so interesting to me, I couldn't put the book down," Tagger replied, anxious to continue.

Mr. Jensen was curious about the extent of Tagger's education and her intellectual capability. He wanted to test her in other areas, but fishing was her livelihood. Better to let her exhaust herself on this subject before they explored others. She finally told him more about her "primary school" education under Gina's tutelage, and he was impressed.

He stepped to the blackboard and began to lecture on other subjects that might interest her. He introduced the subjects of biology, geography and astronomy to whet her appetite for more. The transfer of knowledge in the little schoolroom that night stirred in both of them the classic emotions that teachers and pupils have shared for centuries.

Mr. Jensen so reveled in this pupil that he could have gone on until the wee hours of the morning, but he knew Tagger had to get up early. And she'd been up all night the night before!

"Let's quit for now and start again in two nights," he said finally.

Tagger was disappointed to see the first lesson end, but she didn't want to annoy her professor. He had unlocked a door for her that she never wanted closed again. So she prepared to leave without an argument.

"Is six o'clock Thursday night all right?" Mr. Jensen asked.

"Yes, that's fine. I can't tell you how much I appreciate this. "You will let me pay you," she insisted as she reached for her tagger pouch.

"You already have, Tagger. More than you realize. To see your hunger for knowledge is payment enough."

CHAPTER 22
The Mysteries

The private tutoring continued throughout the fall and into the brutal winter. Despite the snow and bitter cold, Tagger never missed a class session. It always seemed that time passed so slowly between her precious lessons.

They settled into a pattern. Mr. Jensen would give her books, books on every imaginable subject. Once she'd read them, they'd discuss passages from her assignment, and Mr. Jensen would share his knowledge on the subject.

She studied so intensely that one night Mr. Jensen had to speak to her. "Tagger, I know you love to read and study, but you must slow down a bit. You have to maintain a balance in your life, which means that you have to rest too."

She could see that Mr. Jensen was genuinely concerned about her. "I'll try," Tagger promised. "I just can't seem to get enough; there's so much to learn."

He wasn't convinced she would slow down, but on the other hand, he didn't want to hold back anything that made her so happy.

Mr. Jensen had been surprised at how much Tagger had picked up from Gina; he was particularly impressed that she was a bit familiar with many sonnets and plays by Shakespeare. What was even more astounding was her personal life philosophy. She had remarkably advanced notions for a child her age. Like Gina, he sometimes wondered if she knew more about life than he.

In the months that followed, Mr. Jensen acquainted Tagger with the mysteries of mathematics and the sciences and the beauty of literature, the languages and the arts. But most important, he literally inspired her with the wonders of history.

The early explorers intrigued her the most. They were so brave and adventurous. There was Vasco da Gama, the first European to reach India by sea; Henry Hudson, who discovered both a river and a bay in North America; and of course, Christopher Columbus, who sighted land off the coasts of North and South America in his attempt to find a route to India.

But her favorite was the Portuguese explorer Ferdinand Magellan who planned the first voyage to sail around the world. He left Seville, Spain in 1519, with five ships and discovered a passage around the southern tip of South America, which was later named after him—the Straits of Magellan.

Although Magellan was slain before the end of the voyage, one of the ships in his fleet made it back to Seville in 1522, finally proving that it was possible to sail around the world. Tagger admired his courage so, especially when she read that he died valiantly defending his crew against warring natives in the Philippines.

Tagger was awed too by the determined settlers who founded Jamestown, Virginia and Plymouth, Massachusetts, and by the heroic revolutionary patriots, Thomas Jefferson, Benjamin Franklin, Robert Morris, Paul Revere, John

Hancock and Connecticut's own Nathan Hale. Why, even Stonington had its heroes of the War of 1812, men who fended off an attack by a British fleet that was planning to burn the town. She understood now that each of these heroes had risked his life and fortune for the bittersweet taste of liberty in the United States.

"I'm disappointed that there don't seem to be many famous women in history," she said once to Mr. Jensen, when they were studying American history.

"Well, there is some truth to that," Mr. Jensen agreed. "The roles of women were much different then. But think about Queen Isabella, who financed Columbus' voyages and Abigail Adams, who insisted her husband, President John Adams, consider the rights of women. And then there were Ann Austin and Mary Fisher, who suffered prison and banishment when they simply tried to introduce the Quaker religion in Boston. These were all heroines in their own right."

Though the numbers were meager, Tagger was sure more women would step forward in years to come; they would be recognized for their achievements and their courage in their own spheres. Perhaps, in some small way she could be one of them.

"You know, Gina is a brave woman, Mr. Jensen. She's overcome many personal battles to achieve success. It was probably as hard for her to expand her business as it was for Columbus to set off across the Atlantic."

Tagger's cottage stayed warm and dry during the winter. She often ate with Gina, but other times she would cook something over the fireplace coals. As spring neared, the winter days began to turn longer.

Robins and warblers also returned to the forest, glad to rest after their long flight from the south. The bitter winds softened as the gentle sea breezes took their place. The sun's rays glinted on the waves in the harbor, and Tagger was overjoyed. The Andersons often stopped by to make sure that she was safe and healthy. She didn't mind their visits now, for she realized they were decent people concerned about her well-being.

Tagger already knew the teaching sessions had to end in the spring. Mr. Jensen had signed a contract to spend each summer in Gloucester, England, tutoring the children of wealthy aristocrats. A substitute schoolmaster would teach the midsummer session. Tagger dreaded to see Mr. Jensen go, but looked forward to renewing her friendship with Gina.

As she walked along the path to her cottage, one evening, Tagger noticed the green tendrils of grass fighting through the tangle of dead leaves from the previous fall. She was counting her blessings. She had everything a girl could want. Why was it then that something gnawed at her?

CHAPTER 23
The Losses

The distant hoot of an owl in the black-shrouded forest near the schoolhouse distracted Tagger. She'd been listening intently to Mr. Jensen's presentation on the Hundred Years War, but the lonesome sound of the bird depressed her somehow.

"What's bothering you, Tagger?" Mr. Jensen asked, noting the dark shadow of pain in her eyes.

"Nothing really," Tagger answered a little too quickly. "I guess I just have a lot on my mind."

She couldn't discuss her feelings with Mr. Jensen, even though he was so understanding. Her enthusiasm for learning never waned, but sometimes she was so serious that he knew something must be troubling her.

He had seen these same symptoms in so many of his students through the years. Young boys and girls seemed to long for affection from the opposite sex almost before they understood what it meant. It was wonderful to watch their emotions blossom, but it was sad too to see their anxiety. He had been young once too.

It wouldn't be long before Mr. Jensen would be sailing for England. He regretted leaving Tagger. She needed him right now, though she would never discuss her deep, private feelings with him.

His solution was to leave several books for Tagger to read over the summer. He included some classical romances like Homer's *Iliad*, and Shakespeare's *Anthony and Cleopatra* and *Romeo and Juliet*. Maybe she'd see that her feelings were as ageless as those of these fictional characters.

On the day he was to leave for his summer assignment, Tagger went to Mr. Jensen's home to see him off. He lived in a small, cozy cottage near the gristmill. When she arrived, she noticed the shades were drawn and the shutters were closed for the summer. Even though the cottage looked desolate, Mr. Jensen emerged in a cheerful mood. He checked the premises one last time and locked the door.

Tagger carried one of Mr. Jensen's small valises as they sauntered along the path to the harbor. He was a good actor; he made her believe he was excited to go to his summer job. She was a good actress; she made him believe she'd do fine without him.

A sleek sloop with high gunwales and a wooden mast that soared into the clouds above waited in the harbor. This sloop would take him to New York, where he would catch a much larger, square-rigged packet ship that would take him to London.

"It's a good day for sailing," Tagger noted. "The wind is strong, but warm."

The white sails of the sloop snapped back and forth smartly in the sunlight. Tagger wished she could go with Mr. Jensen. When they drew closer to the dock, they could hear the clinking and clanking of the sloop's brass fittings, as the halyards bumped against each other in the breeze.

At the end of the gangway, a young sailor with windblown hair yelled, "Ahoy, Mr. Jensen. All set for the voyage?"

"Yes, I'm ready. Looks like a fine day."

The sailor was coming down the swaying gangway now to collect Mr. Jensen's bags. Balancing the weight of the bags carefully, he headed back up to stow the luggage, leaving Mr. Jensen and Tagger to say their goodbyes.

Mr. Jensen reached out and squeezed Tagger's hand. She stood on tiptoe and kissed his check.

"Take care of yourself, young miss. I'll see you in the fall."

The crew busied themselves with casting off from the dock, and then the sloop set sail. Tagger saw Mr. Jensen on the deck above and waved enthusiastically. He returned the gesture, and she watched until the ship was so far out on the waves that it looked no larger than a toy boat in a washtub.

Weeks passed; spring turned to summer. One day Tagger realized that she hadn't seen Gina for three days. Usually both she and Gina were quite faithful in following the town's instructions for frequent visits, but since Tagger had been going to school, she'd relied upon Diane to deliver the fish and oysters to Gina's shop. Gina understood. She was glad to see Tagger receiving the schooling she needed, so she didn't insist that Tagger come to see her. But she still went to see Tagger several times a week. Why hadn't she been there? Tagger wondered. She must pay her a visit.

As she started toward town the wind picked up suddenly. It wasn't until then that Tagger noticed the dark clouds looming in the southwest. They pushed and fought each other in a wild race across the sky. Dust swirled up from the gravel roads. It was so thick, she had to blink her eyes to see.

She shielded her face and looked in the direction of Gina's

shop. She thought for a moment she saw a "closed" sign in the shop window, but that couldn't be right. She blinked again. It did say, "closed." It was never closed during the morning. She started running now, the pebbles in the dust stinging her face.

A man in work clothes was sweeping up in front of Gina's store. He stopped and looked up. Just then a brisk gust of wind cut across the sensitive nape of his neck. He shivered as Tagger ran up. She was panting, frightened, speaking in spurts.

"Where's, Gina? Who are you? What's happened?" Tagger was almost sobbing.

"Now, now, little lady. I'm afraid it's bad news. The owner, well, she's gone, passed away late last night, she did."

"Nooooo, oh no, it can't be true," Tagger screamed. She reeled; she felt faint. Then she caught herself and with a vengeance, grabbed at the man. In a fit of anger, she beat at his chest with her clenched fists.

"You're wrong, you cruel man. I just saw her three days ago. There was nothing wrong." Her hands had turned to jelly, though, and he barely felt the blows.

He wasn't angry. He had children of his own and understood how she must feel. He gently caught her hands in his and held her until her rage passed.

"I'm sorry," he comforted her. "You must have been very close to the dear lady. Something just went wrong with her heart. The doctor's not sure what it was. She didn't suffer though, went real fast. Ladies from the Mariners Church came and laid her out in her best clothes for burial. They're keeping watch over her until the service tomorrow."

Tagger was racked with sobs. She hadn't even known.

Nobody had thought to notify her. She wanted to lie down in the street and beat the pavement, but she managed to remain upright. It was all she could do to compose herself so she could enter the shop. Her dear friend was lying so quietly; her beautiful face peaceful at rest. Tagger and the ladies from the church kept a vigil throughout the night. The rain came hard at dusk and continued for hours, throughout the night.

"Poor, poor Gina," Tagger kept saying. "She had so much to give, but such a short life." Gina was only thirty-six.

At 7:00 AM the rain stopped, and Tagger dragged herself home to change clothes for the funeral service to be held at 10:00 at the church. She wore the blue dress that she and Gina had made; it was a tribute to her friend. Her hair was long and lustrous now, but her red, swollen eyes detracted from her lovely image.

The newly ordained Unitarian minister, Mr. Harold Evings, gave the eulogy and the short, simple sermon. It was a large gathering. Many of Gina's customers attended, and her two cousins, from the nearby village of Noank, came with their children.

All of the Fish Children were there, dressed in the best clothes they owned. They formed a little group at the back of the crowd afterward, trying to comfort Tagger in her grief, although they were nearly overcome by their own. Renaud held her arm to support her, and Edward watched her face with his sensitive eyes, letting her know he felt the same pain. Tagger was quiet and tried not to cry.

After the service, the mourners met at the grave site. The steady rain flowed again, forming rivulets of water on the surface of the oak coffin. Reverend Evings said a few more words of comfort, and then it was over. Once the coffin was lowered into the gaping, muddy hole, the crowd dispersed quickly.

Diane and the boys tried to get Tagger to leave, but she insisted on being alone with Gina. Finally everyone was gone but her. She fell on her knees in the broken clumps of grass beside the new mound of dirt and burst into tears again, letting her emotions flow.

"Gina, Gina. I had no idea you were so sick. Why didn't you tell me? Maybe I could have gotten you help. Oh, it just can't be true. We had such plans, such dreams. They're all gone now." She was exhausted from the sobbing and from her own questions.

Finally she dragged herself to her feet when the workmen came to fill in the grave. She stumbled back to her cottage, swept along by the wind and rain.

CHAPTER 24
The New Shop Owner

When Tagger woke up late on the morning of the fourth day after Gina's funeral, the storm had passed. The sun had prevailed against the rain and shown through the windows. At first she reveled in the mild weather, and then instantly remembered that she'd lost her dearest friend, her guardian and her colleague. She could not face the day.

Finally she forced herself to sit up, holding her knees with her arms. The chill of loneliness caused her to shiver uncontrollably.

Gina was gone forever. What would she do without her guardian? Would the sheriff force her to live with a family in the village now?

Her life was shattered. The Fish Children would be arriving at the pier at noon, ready to fish, but there would be no one to buy their catch. She needed to be there with them, no matter how hard it was for her to get dressed and ready.

Everyone was there when she finally arrived. She called them together. "Yes, it's true," she started, barely audible at first. "We've lost a wonderful friend and suffered a major setback, as well. But we can't give up. Gina wouldn't have wanted that. And of course I have the problem of guardianship again.

"I think the best thing is for me to see Sheriff Anderson,"

she went on, "before he comes to see me. I saw him at the funeral, so he knows I'm alone again. I'm older now, maybe even eleven, so maybe he won't have to place me in a family."

"Yes, Tagger," Renaud agreed. "You've proven that you can care for yourself." Everyone was silent then. They realized their futures were uncertain too.

Tagger nodded and said, "And there are other merchants in the village who sell fish; surely someone will buy ours." She was the only one who remembered how hard it had been initially to find a buyer.

When she reached the sheriff's house, he told her how sorry he was about Gina and what a wonderful guardian she had been. He was worried. What was he going to do with this strong-willed girl? "Tagger, I think I have an idea."

Tagger held her breath until he spoke again, afraid she'd cry. "Yes," she whispered.

"This is a most unusual situation. According to the law, I have to find a guardian for you, but you're doing well on your own. Gina assured me of that over and over. I don't want to force you to pack up your belongings and move in with strangers. So this is what we'll do. I'll become your guardian until you are of legal age. That way I can fill out the paperwork myself each month and send it up to the county office. My wife and I live close enough, and we will check on you from time to time. If you ever need something or you get sick or hurt, you let me know it right away. We'll see to it that you get the proper care."

When he finished, Tagger stared at him in disbelief. Her mouth dropped open, but no words came out.

Sheriff Anderson broke the silence. With a smile, he said, "Well what d'ya think, Miss Tagger? I don't make this offer to just anyone!"

"Oh, yes, that would be the perfect solution," Tagger said as she let out her breath. She was so relieved as she left the sheriff's office, but what about the fish business they all depended on for their livelihood?

She made a few trips to the other butcher shops in Portersville, but the results were discouraging, as she had expected. Mr. Derek, who seemed to have a great deal of influence over the other store owners, said, "You might as well give up in Portersville. No one will buy your fish here. We all have our own suppliers—adults, who are much more reliable than street urchins."

Tomorrow she'd go north up the Mystic to Head of the River; maybe they'd be more receptive. It would be difficult to get her fish there before they spoiled, but there didn't seem to be any better alternative at the moment.

She was on the way back to the pier to break the good and bad news of the day to her employees, when she noticed a light in Gina's old shop. Suddenly Tagger had an idea.

Maybe if someone bought Gina's shop, they would still use it as a meat market. Maybe they would need a fish supplier. Maybe they would be interested in her good rates.

The other store owners would undoubtedly try to influence the newcomer against Tagger, but it was worth a try. And it was certainly better than doing business in another town.

She paused before the doorway of Gina's shop, the doorway she'd entered so many times before. The shop was empty now, except for the barren counters and tables.

She decided it was best to knock. After some time, the door was opened by the same man who'd been sweeping the sidewalk the day after Gina's death.

"Hello," Tagger said, embarrassed by her behavior the day after Gina had died. "I want to apologize for the way I acted the other day. I was just so shocked about Gina." Her name caught in Tagger's throat as tears began to well up in her eyes.

"I understand, little lady. I heard 'em say at the funeral service that she was your guardian. I reckon I might have done the same if I was a-grievin'.

"My name's Jerome," he offered. "Miss Gina's cousins hired me to clean up the shop, so they could sell it. I heard a man in Mystic Bridge is already interested. It seems he's selling his shop there and wants to move to Portersville. I understand he plans to sell fish, lobsters and oysters as well as meat."

This sounded like a promising development for Tagger and the Fish Children. Maybe he would be her seller.

"His name's Mr. Garth," Jerome continued, seeing Tagger light up with the news. "He should be coming in the next few days to look at the shop."

CHAPTER 25
Mr. Garth

The stream next to the cottage was running clear and cool over the jagged, granite rocks. Tagger sat down gingerly on a ledge and washed herself. She wanted to be clean and fresh for her meeting with the new shop owner, Mr. Garth.

After her bath, she wrapped herself in a big towel. A new plaid dress hung flapping in the westerly breeze on a clothesline she'd suspended between two oaks. She'd only worn it once before, so the colors were still bright. It fit her well, and she loved the way the white collar contrasted with her tanned face.

Tagger had learned that if she tied a rock to the hem of her clothes as they dried, it pulled out the wrinkles. Now that she had money from her business, she'd bought herself cloth to make clothes. If things went well at her meeting, she might even buy the dark red material with the tiny flower print that she'd seen at the notions shop.

Or perhaps she'd buy an iron. She'd seen them at Mr. Markle's. You heated the heavy thing up in the fireplace or on a stove and then ran it across your clothes to flatten the wrinkles.

She put on the dress. It looked smooth and neat, and she thought she presented a good image. But her hair was a mess, going in different directions, totally unmanageable. She combed it several different ways, trying to look more mature, but with little success. Even though she was almost eleven, and maturing quickly, she still looked like a little girl. She had to convince Mr. Garth that she was responsible enough to be his supplier.

When she arrived at Gina's old shop, the door was ajar. How different it was now. She could still smell the faint aroma of the spices Gina always used to preserve her fish and meat, and she could remember the evenings by the fire when Gina had shared her simple knowledge of life with her. The pain of loss gripped her, but she had to be strong now. So much rested on the outcome of this meeting.

He was standing at the counter with his back to the door and hadn't seen her come in.

"Excuse me, Mr. Garth," said Tagger.

The man turned quickly and said, "You must be the young fisher . . ."

He stopped in mid-sentence. They both stared at each other. It was John, the orphan boy she'd met last year in front of the brass shop. Although it had been a while since their brief meeting, she recognized him immediately—his proud demeanor and sincere brown eyes. But he was totally confused.

"I'm Tagger," she smiled, watching his reaction. "I met you at the brass shop. How are you, John?"

"Yes, I remember, but, but, you were a . . ." he stammered.

"A boy," she finished for him. "Yes, I was alone, and I didn't want anyone to know I was a girl. But now I'm a ward of the town, so everyone knows I'm really a girl."

"I see," he murmured, still trying to adjust to the change.

"How glad I am to see you. I'd planned to find you, Tagger, except I was looking for a young man. I didn't know I would find such an attractive young lady. How are you?"

"I'm fine," she replied, flustered by the compliment. She couldn't keep from staring at him. In just a little more than a year he had grown into a strikingly handsome young man. He was tall with broad shoulders, and she could see the long, smooth muscles of his forearms, exposed under his rolled shirt sleeves.

The strangest feeling came over her. It wasn't unpleasant, but she couldn't explain it—it was sort of a spreading warmth. But she remembered she was here on business and quickly snapped back to the reality of the situation.

With the shock of their meeting over now, it was time to catch up. John went first.

"When I left Portersville the day I met you, I went to Mystic Bridge and hired on as a fisherman with a large fleet owned by the Dickson brothers. We brought in large hauls of cod and halibut." John looked directly into Tagger's eyes the whole time he talked.

"The job lasted a couple of months," he continued. "It was tough work, but the pay was good. Soon after, I hired on with the big whaling ship, the *Thomas Ellington*.

"We hunted whales in the South Atlantic for two months, but I hated it when we made a kill. I kept telling myself how important the whale oil was for lamps and to lubricate machinery, but it was still terrible to see those poor creatures die. The only good thing was that our crew was so successful. We all received large shares from the profits, and fortunately, it was the last time I had to go whaling.

"In the spring, I took my little stash of money and opened

a small butcher shop in Mystic Bridge. It was slow going at first because I had a lot to learn, but gradually I built it into a fairly respectable business. It helped that my parents had taught me to read, write and cipher a bit. When I heard that Gina's store was for sale here in Portersville and that it was larger than mine, I jumped at the chance to buy it. I hoped I might even see you again when I returned." His brilliant smile lit the room, "Only not as a girl!"

"I'm so happy for you, John," Tagger smiled back. "You certainly did well in such a short time."

John was happy for Tagger too when she brought him up to date on her life, and he realized she'd come a long way from the poor little boy he'd known earlier. He was sad to hear that Tagger had lost her friend Gina, but he was glad it was he who replaced her.

By the end of Tagger's visit, she and John had reached a business arrangement that would benefit them both. He would buy all the fish she could provide and pay her one cent per pound. John wrote out a little note on a scrap of paper desribing their arrangement, and they both signed it. Tagger bid John good-day and hurried off to tell the Fish Children.

CHAPTER 26
The Determined

The months and seasons rolled along comfortably now. Tagger and the Fish Children were slowly adjusting to the loss of Gina, although they would never forget what she had meant to them. The arrangement with John was working well, and Tagger was easily meeting her needs for food, clothing and shelter. Her business was clearly flourishing, and she passed her twelfth, then thirteenth and fourteenth birthdays; although she didn't know exactly what day her birthday was.

The villages along both sides of the Mystic River were growing too. The existing shipyards increased their production of ships, while new yards sprang up to compete with them. Charles Mallory invested the profits he'd made from a sail loft into a growing fleet of whaling ships that sailed to every corner of the Atlantic. Trade with the south increased as cotton became more and more profitable, and southerners were able to ship in more manufactured products from the north. Steamboats and the railroad came to the area as well.

Fishing and shipbuilding thrived in Noank too. In 1831 a lighthouse was built on Morgan Point at the mouth of the Mystic River and guided the many ships that passed into the harbor.

Tagger was a wise businesswoman. The year that she

turned fifteen, she set a goal at the beginning of the year to buy a fishing boat and started right then to save her money. John began to salt some of the Fish Children's catch each week and sold it to several ports south of the Mystic area.

Tagger's guiding principle always kept her pushing ahead. She knew she had to make some sacrifices in the present in order to have what she wanted in the future. Soon the time would come when she would have enough money to buy a boat.

One day in early July, when she guessed herself to be about sixteen, she knew the time was right. She set off to begin her search for the right boat. It wasn't hard to find a shipyard. The Mystic River had become famous for wooden shipbuilding, with the shipyards producing everything from rowboats to three-masted schooners. She would have no problem finding a boat once she knew what she needed, or rather, what she and the Fish Children could handle.

It was fun just to walk through the shipyards and watch the builders cut and fashion the wood that would eventually become the powerful sloops and schooners that plunged through the water. She carefully studied their structural lines, the types of wood they used, and most of all, the quality and size of the sails. She loved the smell of sawdust and fresh paint, so these visits were more pleasure than business.

The townspeople were getting used to the fact that Tagger was a serious businesswoman, albeit a young one. They could easily see she had money to spend, so the owners of the boatyards welcomed her. Each of them had his own sales tactics, and everyone she talked to encouraged her to part with the precious money she'd saved.

Tagger was at the Leeds Shipyard at Head of the River

one day, looking at a new sloop that had just been built by a proud crew of builders. Three of the paint-covered fellows were standing around the boat, congratulating themselves for their fine craftsmanship, while Tagger looked on.

Just as she turned to leave, she saw Mary, who had happened by. As always, Tagger was delighted to see her. Their meetings were infrequent, but she always learned so much from Mary, when she could get her to stay long enough to talk.

"What are you up to now?" Mary asked, peering through squinted eyes for a better look at Tagger.

"Oh Mary. I'm so glad I ran into you. I'm shopping for a fishing boat, but I'm confused by all the different types. I'm not sure what to look for."

In her usual reluctant manner, Mary began to volunteer some advice about fishing craft. "Well you need to consider the size of the deck where you'll land the fish, the device you use for bringing in the lobster pots, the draft of the hull." Tagger began to get lost in many details she'd never thought of. "I'll help you if you wish," Mary offered.

"How do you know so much about boats?" Tagger asked.

"Oh, I guess I know a little bit about everything involved with fishing," Mary answered, a slight smile creeping across her usually somber face. She looked so much younger when she smiled.

It was late July when Tagger made her decision. She and Mary were standing on a sun-bleached dock at the mouth of the harbor, leaning against the brisk wind.

They stared appraisingly at the *Sassy Susan* bobbing against her moorings. It was as though unspoken words passed between them. They looked at each and nodded at the same time. The boat was perfect, except for that terrible name.

The boat of Tagger's dreams turned out to be a proud, but practical smack, a type of one-masted sloop. It belonged to Mr. Langly, a hard-working waterman.

The seasoned boat had served him well, and now he was retiring from the trade. He loved the craft, which he had named for his wife who was deceased now, and had cared for it faithfully. Tagger was sorry she'd made sport of the name, if only to Mary; she hadn't realized it held a special meaning for Mr. Langly.

It wasn't a sleek vessel like the pleasure boats on the bay, but it was sturdy and functional, about thirty feet long with a shallow draft.

A hoist fixed to the starboard side was used to bring in long trawls of lobster pots. The smooth wooden deck was broad and sloping, so that when the sea water shipped over the sides, it could drain back without flooding the boat. About midships, there was a well in the deck where the catch could be stored until the boat returned to shore.

Best of all, the single mast was expertly positioned, so the large sails would whisk the boat along in even the lightest of breezes. The boat was fifteen years old, but the hull was sturdy and the patched sails were seaworthy.

Mr. Langly liked Tagger and Mary and felt they would maintain the *Sassy Susan* properly. He doubted they could afford the price he was asking, though, and he really needed the cash for his move to a warmer climate.

He didn't worry for long. After they'd negotiated a price, Tagger promptly produced a roll of bills from her tagger pouch. She quickly counted out the exact amount they'd agreed upon.

Mr. Langly gaped at the bills as they fluttered into his hand. For a moment he was speechless. Then he said, "Oh, I see. Your grandmother, here, is letting you play like you're buying the boat." He winked at Mary to show her he was in on the game. Mary smiled back, but shook her head.

"No," Tagger said firmly. "I'm buying it for my fishing business. Mary is my friend. I don't have a grandmother."

"I remember now," Mr. Langly said, scratching his shaggy head. "I've heard about you, little lady. You're the orphan who started your own business when everyone thought you were a boy. Is that right?"

"Yes it is." Tagger was pleased that people had heard of her and the business. "My name's Tagger," she said as she nodded to him respectfully. She and Mary stepped aboard her new purchase and began untying lines.

"Good luck, lass. Take good care of the *Sassy Susan* for me, will ya' please."

"I will," Tagger called back through the wind as she and Mary floated out into the bay. Tagger thought she saw some pain in Mr. Langly's eyes as his old friend carried a new captain out for her first adventure. But Mr. Langly must have known that Tagger was sincere; the Sassy Susan would be well cared for.

It was only as the boat pounded through the waves that Tagger became aware of its massive size. She was awed and dwarfed, not just by the boat, but by the power of the ocean. This was the first time she'd actually been out on the water.

Tagger had always watched the ocean from a safe distance before. Mary sensed her apprehension, and with a reassuring smile said, "Just be calm. Go with the roll of the boat."

Tagger relaxed a little and sat back against the gunwale.

She knew she'd be safe with Mary.

During the rest of the afternoon, Mary instructed Tagger on how to sail the sloop. Though Mary's eyesight was poor, she could still see shape and light, but objects were fairly blurry to her. Between the two of them, they got by.

The hardest part for Tagger was raising and setting the sails, because that required some strength. Tagger had to hold tight to the gunwale as she raised the mainsail. The force of the wind flapped the billowing white sails against her and almost swept her off the deck.

"This is harder than I thought, Mary. I hope the Fish Children and I can handle the boat."

"You'll be all right," Mary assured her. "You youngsters are about the most determined people I've ever seen."

First Mary showed Tagger how to sail in the same direction with the wind and then against it, tacking back and forth, but in a forward motion. Then she had Tagger take the tiller and maneuver back and forth across the harbor until she saw her gain confidence in herself.

Next, she showed Tagger how to sail into the wind, so the boat would slow when it was time to throw the trawl out. Then Mary showed her how to drag the trawl and the lobster pots in with the hoist while the sails were luffing. The next step was to quickly stow the catch in the cool water of the well before the sun scorched it.

It didn't take Tagger long to learn the basics; Mary was amazed. But Tagger was worried too. Could she and the Fish Children handle this craft and still catch fish and lobsters with it?

Turning toward the shore, an idea was unfolding for Tagger. Maybe, just maybe, Mary would captain her ship and her crew. That way Tagger would be able to spend more time watching over the catch. She'd been wondering how she was going to sail the ship and make sure they landed the catch at the same time.

Mary could be the answer. She would have to be careful though. Mary was proud and independent and reluctant to become involved with others.

The Fish Children shouted with delight as Tagger and Mary sailed up to the fishing pier. "Is it yours?" Renaud called out before they landed.

"It's ours," Tagger corrected. "We've all earned it."

Everyone started jumping up and down in excitement. After she'd secured the boat to the pilings, they hopped aboard to explore. The boat bounced and shifted with the new weight.

Diane and Renaud ran up to Tagger as soon as they climbed onto the pier and volunteered to serve as crew. Before she could answer, Edward clambered out of the boat and begged to be part of the crew as well.

"You know," Tagger said laughing. "I think we'll all need to serve as crew, at least for a while; sailing this boat will be quite an undertaking for a bunch of landlubbers."

As she said this, she saw Mary hurrying down the pier to the shore. By now the animated Fish Children had crowded around Tagger, all talking at once. Tagger strained on tiptoe to look over their heads to see which way Mary was going. She excused herself apologetically and ran off in the direction Mary had headed.

By the time Tagger caught up to her, Mary was deep into the woods. The coolness of shade from the dense trees made a pleasant contrast to the scorching sun on the water. Tagger was happy they had come together here. She felt more confident in the protective shade.

Tagger was panting a bit as she approached Mary. "I didn't have a chance to thank you," she said sincerely.

"That's all right. Not necessary. You were busy." Mary continued along the path to town with Tagger in tow.

"No, wait. Can't you stay just for a moment?" Tagger rushed after Mary, stepping ahead of her on the path.

"What d'ya want now, you little pest?" But she was smiling, and Tagger felt relieved.

"Well," said Tagger slowly, "I . . . I need some more help. I've bothered you enough, but I have one more favor."

Mary didn't move away, and she remained silent. She was waiting.

"I need someone to help with the business, someone like you who can sail a fishing boat. And I need a captain who can teach the others to work together as a crew."

The old woman didn't speak for a moment, and her face was expressionless. Tagger felt an eternity pass while she waited for her response.

She tried another tack. "I need you Mary. You've got the experience I need. I could pay you a percentage of the catch. It may not be much at first, but I'll give you all I can. You can see how much this means to me."

"I can't see much of anything anymore," Mary laughed bitterly.

"The crew and I will be your eyes," Tagger replied seriously. "All you have to do is tell them what you told me."

Finally Mary spoke. "Why would I want to work for you? I got my own fishin' business." She was gruff but not hostile, and Tagger capitalized on this.

"I'll tell you why you should, Mary, because I need you; people need each other! You've got a talent I can use, and I can pay you for it. We'll have each other. Think about it, please. I'll be waiting for your answer."

Mary stalked off after gently pushing Tagger aside. "Work for you," she mumbled, "fine thing that'd be."

Tagger announced that she would need everyone to accompany her on the maiden voyage the next afternoon. This was followed by shouts of joy.

While they were stowing the gear, Diane suddenly stopped and looked at Tagger. "We don't have a new name for the smack. We can't go out until we have our own name," she said as though it were a statement of fact.

Tagger agreed. "Yes, we must have a new name. I don't think the late Miss Susan would mind having her name retired."

"What do you think about calling her *Determined?*" Diane suggested. "It seems to fit us." They all agreed at once.

"Edward, would you please paint over the *Sassy Susan* and replace it with *Determined?*"

Their first day out bordered on catastrophe, with Edward nearly falling out of the boat when he tried to bring in the lobster pots. Diane and Renaud had been hand lining over the gunwhales and did manage to bring in a small catch of cod, but they lost several fish as the boat lurched in the waves. Fishing from a boat required a completely different technique. They needed more instruction as well as practice. How could Tagger work with them while she was trying to maneuver and steady the boat?

"We can't give up now," she said. "We've never given up before."

When they were within sight of the pier, she unconsciously began scanning the shoreline, hoping Mary would be there. There was no sign of her.

Tagger was disappointed. She was still hoping Mary would accept her offer.

Tomorrow would be better. Surely.

The next day, the sun was at noontide when Tagger arrived at the pier. While she waited for the others to finish their morning duties, she felt the sun was there just for her—to warm and encourage her. A moderate wind kept the crests of the waves low. All the signs were right for a good day.

When they had sailed out to the lobster pots, it was time to bring in the trawl, and she brought the boat about smoothly. Renaud and Diane pulled in the pots which contained a few lively lobsters. Between the lobsters and the catch caught with the fishing lines, the well was about half full when it was time to sail back.

"Yes, this was definitely a better day," Diane said as she swung onto the long wooden seat where Tagger was perched, steering with the long tiller. But she could see that Tagger still had misgivings.

"Each day will be better," she promised Diane with her best smile. "We can do it. It's just one more challenge to face."

But what really worried Tagger was their safety. What if the weather turned bad suddenly? Could she handle the boat under rough seas? She would never forgive herself if one of her trusting employees was injured or fell overboard.

Even after she'd learned to sail herself, Tagger would have to teach someone else too—maybe Diane or Renaud, because eventually she'd have to spend more time tending to other parts of her business.

It was a lovely evening that night as Tagger headed home after delivering the catch. The moon was shining through the thick trees. A warm, gentle breeze flushed the leaves, creating a fluttering pattern of shadows across the hardened dirt path. The cottage was dark as she approached, but moonlight shown on a figure sitting on the doorstep. Tagger wasn't frightened; she knew who it was—who it had to be.

When she was directly in front of the seated figure, she realized she was holding her breath in anticipation. She almost gasped in relief as she said, "Good evening, Mary. Come inside and I'll fix you some tea."

Without moving, Mary spoke slowly as though she had given a lot of thought to the few words that followed. "Tagger . . . I've come to accept your offer. I'll sail your boat."

CHAPTER 27
The Scary Feelings

Tagger was enjoying the business relationship with John and believed that he did too. Lately she'd taken to coming at the end of the week after the shop closed. If it was warm, they'd sit on the back porch and sip tea. John would roast bits of meat to munch on and bring out bread and mustard while they carried on their business transaction.

The strangest part about their weekly meetings was that they both felt charged emotionally afterwards. John had huge bursts of energy. Once he worked late into the night rearranging all the counters, he admitted to Tagger. Another time, he built an oak counter with shelves and glass windows.

Tagger always stimulated his mind, and because of her encouragement, John was able to formulate his plans for expansion. Before he'd gotten to know her, they'd only been fleeting thoughts.

Tagger, on the other, was simply puzzled by her feelings. Why did she feel like jumping across a brook or climbing a mountain? Why was she so confused, yet so excited?

She read and reread the books Mr. Jensen had left with her several summers ago. They were comforting. Through them, she learned that her thoughts weren't so unusual.

The characters in Shakespeare's plays behaved rather

strangely sometimes in the presence of the opposite sex. Romeo and Juliet were distraught whenever they met, and many other characters had similar unexplained reactions.

But still, Tagger was a little concerned. When John was around, she seemed to lose control of her feelings, at least temporarily. This was a new and frightful experience for her, because she had always prided herself in keeping her emotions in check.

Tagger waited eagerly for Mr. Jensen to return to Mystic this fall, but she doubted she could discuss these new developments with him. He was her last hope though; there were no other adults she trusted enough to confide her weaknesses—at least she thought of them as weaknesses.

It was important for Tagger to keep up a positive image for her employees. They seemed to admire her so much, and they looked up to her as their model. But she was wrong to believe they couldn't accept her weaknesses. They appreciated her as much when times were bad as when they were good.

It was Diane who finally came to Tagger to find out what was wrong. Mary and the Fish Children were packing up their gear for the night when Diane noticed Tagger fidgeting with a fishing line.

The sun was setting and the red glow of dusk lit Tagger's face. A deep frown creased her brow. Quietly, Diane moved to Tagger's side, took the line, and held Tagger's hands in hers.

"What's wrong, Tagger? Please tell me; you seem so unhappy and distant. Are you ill?"

The tears welled up in Tagger's eyes, but she fought them back. "No, nothing's wrong," she replied with a forced smile. "I'm fine, just a little tired, maybe."

But Diane persisted, and Tagger finally opened up. She

slowly revealed her most private emotions of the past few weeks.

"I'm so flustered when I'm with John, and I always behave so stupidly, but when we're apart, I can barely think of anything but him. I enjoy being with him, but when we're together, I get tongue-tied. I sound like a crazy loon. Oh Diane, I don't understand what's wrong with me; I'm usually so calm with the local businessmen."

Diane reflected on Tagger's words for a moment, studied her face and said, "I don't have any education, but I am older than you, and I think I understand your problem. I think you're in love, Tagger! I'm in love too. I'm being courted by Nicholas, the apprentice at the cobbler's shop. We plan to marry someday when we both have saved some money."

"Diane, I didn't realize you were being courted," Tagger said smiling and reaching out to hug her. "I am so happy for you." Perhaps Diane was right. Love was something to think about.

CHAPTER 28
Spindrift

There weren't enough hours in the day for Tagger. She'd been working constantly throughout the long dog days of summer. She bought better equipment, came up with better ways to increase the catches, and constantly planned for the next expansion.

Often she'd go out on *Determined* to help with the trawls and hand lines. She paced the dock continually making sure that all went smoothly and then collapsed in her bed each night, too exhausted to even think of John.

She learned that John's business was growing too, but she only saw him occasionally. Diane was handling his account now.

Tagger had decided to delegate John's account to Diane when it became clear that she just didn't have the time to dally at his shop each week. Business first. Diane didn't question Tagger's decision.

Mr. Jensen returned in the fall from his tutoring position in England, armed with new books, and Tagger's lessons began again. Throughout the winter, Tagger maintained her rigorous schedule—lots of work and study, but little time for rest.

In the spring, when Mr. Jensen set sail for his summer job

again, he begged Tagger to relax and get away from her
business for awhile. She did—for two days. But during her
little vacation, all she could do was think about her next
project.

She was going to have a warehouse built near the pier! The
warehouse would serve as an office and a place to store the
ever-increasing equipment they were acquiring. She'd been
thinking about it for some time, but she knew it was going
to be another big challenge.

Her first test was to find a reliable construction company.
Again she had the problem of being a young girl. She was
gaining respect in the village, but what adult firm would want
to work for her?

Not surprisingly, the owner of the first carpentry group,
Joe Shuster, scoffed at her request. And then the following
day, the manager of Elsbeth and Sons Builders waved her
off before she could even tell them what she wanted. But as
usual, she didn't give up; she was getting used to these
setbacks by now.

Finally, Tagger found a fledgling company named Joiner
Brothers, which was happy to have the business. The builders,
Patrick and Hank, were only a little older than Tagger and
since they were just starting out, they couldn't be too choosy
about their clients. Besides, they immediately liked Tagger
and her fresh, new ideas.

After they'd negotiated the financial part of the
undertaking, they were all ready to begin construction. By
late spring, the framing was nearly up, and it looked as though
the building would be completed before cold weather.

Patrick and Hank worked steadily, and Tagger was pleased
she'd chosen them. The three of them shared a common

bond—a pride in their work and a need to do the best job possible.

Patrick was the older of the two builders and a little more serious. He sported a full blond beard and loved to stroke it slowly when he talked. He reminded Tagger of a Greek philosopher in work clothes. Hank was taller and slimmer, with curly brown hair and an impish grim; he was constantly in motion and loved a good prank now and then.

When she could afford the time, Tagger would slog through the mud and watch the construction; she wished she could help. Building was such a noble profession, she thought. You could immediately see the results of your efforts, and the remarkable thing about it was that the product lasted for decades.

Patrick and Hank had fitted and nailed the frame together as if by magic. Suddenly there was the skeleton of a building where previously there'd been just a bare spot of sandy soil.

They built the door frame large enough to accommodate the fish carts, two of them now, and the growing number of pieces of fishing equipment. A corner in the right front section was partitioned off for her office.

Her office! It was a dream come true. It was more than just a token of success; it was a sign of permanency, of a future. The business was a reality now, solid, tangible. But it needed a name.

When the Fish Children gathered to watch the construction, it was Edward who quietly offered the name that would be used during their generation and generations to come. "I think we should call it Spindrift—Spindrift Company."

Quiet fell over the group as they thought about the

significance of the word. Then they gleefully shouted their agreement. "That's it," they said in unison.

Mary had taught them the word "spindrift" when she'd first accepted her position as *Determined's* captain. Tagger remembered the day only too well. She had wanted the other members of her crew to learn how to sail, so everyone piled into the smack to hear Mary's instructions at the same time.

They sailed back and forth across the bay while Mary demonstrated how to tack into the wind, how to come about safely and how to slow the boat when it was time to bring in the trawl. These were the maneuvers they would need to perform with precision if they were ever to take control of the smack themselves.

Everyone was attentive. They moved quickly from port to starboard and from bow to stern as instructed. The warm, sea air filled them with joy, and they smiled to each other when they passed in the boat.

Tagger was no less excited. Although she had already had her lessons, she was learning more too. She followed Mary's orders obediently, pulling lines, tightening winches and unfurling sails.

They sailed out of the sound into open waters. *Determined* plunged rhythmically up and down into the waves. The wind propelled them forward as though they were being swept along on a big rocking horse. And then, without warning, the skies blackened and the waves began to break with greater force. The waves came more and more often now too, and the roar was deafening.

Salt water splashed over the deck. When it hit, the Fish Children panicked. Diane screamed and Renaud clutched at lines and the mast.

Mary was calm and shouted orders in a firm manner. They responded as best they could. Finally, they all brought the boat to the proper angle against the pounding waves.

Soon the Fish Children could see that although the wind had taunted them with its fearsome strength, *Determined* was clearly under Mary's control. They knew they were safe now, but they still didn't trust the rampaging waves.

The boat settled into a rocking pattern of up and down plunges followed by a violent twist with each downward thrust. The sail fittings thumped and clanked against the wooden mast. As they crested, some of the waves threw off a delicate spray of white droplets into the air.

"It's called spindrift," Mary explained. "When the waves reach a peak like that, the wind catches the crest and blows a stream of water into the air. It seems like the wave rejects an unwanted part of itself. Sometimes when I see the spindrift, it reminds me of the way society casts out those who don't fit in. But remember, the spray flies high into the air—proud and strong and leaves the rest of the wave to churn to its end."

The young people understood, and did not forget that day in the storm or the message they learned. And, when they had to approve the new name of their business, Spindrift Company seemed just right.

CHAPTER 29
The Kiss

The glass panes hadn't been put into the window frames yet, but the lowering sun shown brilliantly on the opposite wall of Tagger's office, a dazzling display. It was late on a Thursday afternoon, and Tagger had lingered at the warehouse as Patrick and Hank packed up their gear for the day.

Often they met to talk in the quiet of the late afternoon. Tonight they all decided to walk down to the beach. As they talked, Tagger learned that each of the Joiner Brothers had a goal, or maybe it was more like a dream. "My goal is to build five buildings in one year," Patrick said. He was kneeling in the damp sand as he talked, busily working it with his fingers, building an elaborate sandcastle.

Hank had stared dreamily beyond the waves and said, "My dream is to save enough money to build a seaworthy ship and sail 'round the world."

They both turned to Tagger, anxious to hear what she would say, but she was silent. She admired them because they knew what would make them happy. She only knew that something would make her happy, but she wasn't sure what. She had everything she'd ever worked for—didn't she?

Her cottage was warm and dry now, but she would soon need a new house, a true home. It just seemed extravagant to rebuild when her place was adequate. Maybe that's what separated her from true happiness; she was still alone, and the ivy-covered home only seemed to be a remote dream.

When the brothers were gone, she returned to her office. She was deep in thought when she suddenly heard the sound of footsteps. The sun was settling deep into the woods now, and an eerie twilight replaced the dancing shadows. She felt a chill. The footsteps came closer. Probably Patrick or Hank, returning for a forgotten tool.

No, to her surprise, it was John. He emerged into the clearing from around the north side of the construction. His tall figure nearly filled the doorway as she motioned him into her office. It had been several weeks since they had really talked.

"What a building!" he exclaimed. "I'd call it a factory rather than a warehouse. Did you design it yourself?"

"Why, yes, I did." Tagger answered. "I wanted something practical but comfortable. We really needed a permanent place."

John marveled at her ingenuity as he surveyed the layout. "You've thought of every detail, Tagger. Why don't you show me the rest."

"All right," she said eagerly. "You'll be my first tour."

He followed her along a small aisle, between plastered walls, trying to take it all in. She pointed as she walked and explained proudly, "This area over here is where we'll put the smaller pieces of equipment— you know, the buckets, carts, extra winches."

She'd had Patrick and Hank build ramps between the two areas for easy loading and unloading. One section of the side wall near the door was equipped with large pegs for storing tools and *Determined*'s sails and lines.

"These are good ideas," John said enthusiastically as he walked around the structure with Tagger. He'd been noticing the excellent workmanship that had gone into both the construction of the building and the interior cabinetry.

They stepped over a few remaining cut boards as they made their way back to her office. It was large and open, with built-in shelves and storage closets.

"It's hard to believe I'll actually have my own office," Tagger mused, enjoying John's company and slowly losing her shyness. Laughing merrily she said, "Now I won't have to do my paperwork on the kitchen table."

"I can just see you sitting there behind a big desk in a nice leather chair. Have you given the company a name yet?"

"Spindrift Company," Tagger announced immediately. Then she explained why the word "spindrift" conveyed such a strong meaning to her and her employees.

"What a clever idea, Tagger. It says so much about all of you. You've worked hard and now you have something of your own, and you've helped the others so much too. Many people never accomplish in a lifetime what you have right now."

She didn't tell him how shy she felt at that moment.

They stood facing each other now in the slowly fading sunlight. A crisp breeze blew through Tagger's tousled hair causing it to brush against her cheeks. They looked deep into each other's eyes.

Tagger was almost squinting—afraid to let John see too much into her. They both felt some ill-defined need—a need to share their feelings at the same time they felt a need to flee.

Without realizing it, they had eased closer to each other. Slowly, almost clumsily, John reached out to brush away a curl that had fallen onto Tagger's brow.

He pulled her to him and their lips met and held. For the rest of what seemed like a lifetime, they stood together, the wind enhancing this new miracle. They couldn't be sure when it happened, but at some precise moment, they both discovered happiness in their first kiss.

CHAPTER 30
The Invitation

Work never seemed so easy or so enjoyable over the next couple of weeks. Tagger floated around the nearly-finished warehouse, rearranging shelving, modifying the placement of the walls and doors, designing more ramps and countertops. She was tireless. Hank and Patrick were awed by her energy.

Tagger came through the wide, double doors, smiling and carrying a bouquet of wild fall flowers, purple asters. She found a long green glass bottle with some water in it and stuffed the stems into the small hole. Walking back through the side door to her office, she placed them on her new wooden desk.

The effect of the bouquet was perfect. It immediately created a homey look in the midst of the raw, unfinished construction.

"There, aren't they lovely?" Tagger said cheerfully. "Flowers do so much to brighten a room. Now let's get on with that counter by the storage room. We still have a couple of hours before dark."

Hank and Patrick just smiled at each other as they hurried after her. But if she had listened closely, she would have heard Patrick complaining about how late it was and how hungry he was getting.

It didn't take long to design the oak counter near the storage room. Patrick had to admit she had a good idea. The counter had folding doors below, which could be opened all the way back to make way for the large buckets they used to transport the fresh fish.

They were brushing the sawdust from their hands when Tagger finally thanked them for the hard day they'd put in. "Go home and eat, you two. Sorry I kept you so long."

"We'll see you tomorrow," Hank called back as the builders headed down the dirt path in the direction of the village. "Get some rest yourself, Tagger; you've been pushing yourself pretty hard."

"All right, if you say so. I have all kinds of ideas for tomorrow."

A few moments later, there was a sound in the woods and Tagger looked up just as John was coming up the path.

"John, is it you?" Tagger's voice was as soft as a breath of wind.

"Yes, I just closed the shop and thought I'd stop by to see you. I can see you've been keeping the Joiners busy. You've made a lot of progress since I was here before. When do you think you'll move in?"

"In about three weeks, I think. I want to move in before the weather turns foul. I'm getting eager."

"Do you think you could take a little time off your project tomorrow. I'd like to talk with you. Can we take a picnic out on the beach or under that big maple tree in the meadow?"

"I know, John, why don't we go out in the smack? The crew is busy on the dock tomorrow, so they won't need *Determined*. Let's sail out into the sound and eat there. You've never been sailing with me."

John smiled widely. "I'll be here at noon. I'll bring the food."

CHAPTER 31
The Noonday Dinner

It was a day to remember: clear, crisp and alive with the smells of early fall. She looked in her small looking glass as she brushed her dark curls. Was she considered pretty, she wondered. Her features were regular and similar to those of other girls, but she wasn't sure what people considered to be pretty. She'd started to fill out a bit, and her body was taking on a rounded, feminine look.

Grabbing her basket she headed for the front of the warehouse, swinging it back and forth. She felt happy, but a little part of her was still guarded, still a little afraid of being hurt.

There was a sawhorse near the big double doors, and she climbed aboard to wait for John. She looked like a toddler on a hobbyhorse.

When John came up the path, he was somber, but as soon as he saw her, his whole face broke into a smile. Obviously he was delighted by the way she looked.

He grabbed her hand and off they went to *Determined*. It was moored at the dock, and Tagger hopped around the sloped deck, swiftly untying the lines and maneuvering the sails into the right position to be lofted.

She asked John to get in and sit on the port side, so she would have room to raise the sails. She pushed off as she jumped in, pointing the bow at an angle to the wind.

The sails began to luff as she quickly pulled the halyard, which raised the mainsail to the top of the mast. She tightened the line around a brass cleat and moved to the bow to set the jib. The boat was moving swiftly out from the shore now.

As she worked the sails, she saw John's face out of the corner of her eye. He was enjoying the moment. Finally she sat down, opposite him on the starboard side of the smack, smiling confidently. They were on their way. The breeze was refreshing, the air clear.

They sailed straight out from the shore for several moments until Tagger turned the boat northward. It was clear she had a place in mind for their picnic, so John waited to be surprised.

After a few minutes, it came into sight off the port bow, a calm little lagoon, tucked away behind a jutting rock cliff. Tagger maneuvered the boat expertly, and soon they were anchored about twenty yards off shore.

They raised the built-in table, which had been battened to the deck while they were sailing and spread their little feast. John had brought several different cold meats and cheeses and a long loaf of white bread. Tagger added the smoked fish and the apricots she'd brought, and before long, they were munching contentedly on the tasty meal.

The boat bobbed up and down slowly in the sparkling waves, creating the sensation of a big rocking chair. They relaxed in each other's company.

After they'd finished sampling all the food, they packed up the uneaten meat and began throwing small pieces of the leftover bread out on the waves. Within minutes there were a dozen white sea gulls, all hovering and squawking at each other and diving for the morsels.

"You know, Tagger, I'm like you," John said. "I was young when I lost my parents and I never had a chance to go to school again after they died. Luckily I had already learned to read and do a little arithmetic before I quit, but it wasn't enough. I've been thinking lately that maybe I should try to get a better education like you are. I was wondering if maybe I could go to school at night, with you. Do you think Mr. Jensen would teach me, too? But I insist on paying him. It would be too much for me to expect him to do this without compensation."

"Oh John, I'm sure he wouldn't mind," Tagger replied with a broad smile. "You'll like him, and I'm sure he'll like you. I'll be glad to introduce you. School will be starting soon. I'm looking forward to seeing him again, too. And I was just thinking that I must insist he take payment this year. He's been so kind to tutor me for nothing, but I'm quite able to pay him now."

John let out a sigh of relief. "Good. I've been afraid to ask you, for fear I'd intrude on you and Mr. Jensen."

"Don't be silly John. I'll enjoy classes even more now. We can learn together."

CHAPTER 32
The Conversation

Just as she expected, Mr. Jensen was sitting at his large wooden desk at the front of the classroom, reading. He hadn't changed much, except that he seemed a bit older and his eyes looked a little tired. She asked him about his summer.

"Oh, it was pretty much the same. England was lovely as usual, and the children I tutored were little scalawags, as usual—too much time spent hunting and dining on over-rich foods. Their parents always have such high hopes for them, but I wonder if they'll even be able to make a living when they're grown. They just don't seem to have much enthusiasm for learning."

She told him of her new warehouse and the growth of the business, and then she got to the real matter on her mind. "I have a favor to ask you this year," she began. "The young man I sell my fish to, John Garth, wants to learn too. He's an orphan and doesn't have much education. He's excited about the possibility of coming with me. Could we include him in our sessions?" Her eyes were pleading, and Mr. Jensen immediately understood the importance of this boy to her. He agreed at once. Reluctantly he accepted the fee they insisted upon paying him.

"May we start tomorrow night?" Tagger asked finally. She was as eager as John.

"That will be fine. I'll see you both at six o'clock."

It was barely daylight when Tagger reached the warehouse the next day. She wanted to make a list for Hank and Patrick, to remind them of a few things that needed to be done today. That way she could attend to other matters.

When the two joiners arrived, she could hear them cracking jokes and jostling each other as they came up the path. She quickly explained what she wanted done and then left them to work at their own pace. She spent the morning at her new desk catching up on the paperwork she'd been putting off.

At noon, she went to the pier. She wanted to check in on her employees, but she knew they would be working well under Diane's able supervision.

Renaud was the first one to hurry over when he saw her arrive. He was becoming a handsome young man. He still had the impish grin and boyish looks, but he was growing taller and was developing a strong, muscular body. He seemed to thrive on hard work and his admiration for Tagger.

"Good day," he said cheerily. "We haven't seen you in ages. How's the warehouse coming? Will we be movin' in soon?"

Tagger smiled warmly at Renaud. "Yes, it's nearly done. I'd say we can move in within the next three weeks."

"When do we have the celebration party, Tagger?" Renaud asked.

"Will there be room for all our gear?" asked Diane.

"Will we have a place to eat our noonday dinner when it's

cold out?" This last question came from the tall and very slender Edward who never seemed to gain an ounce no matter how much he ate.

Tagger answered the questions as best she could and then talked to Diane a while about how they would move the equipment when the time came. When she was satisfied that all was going well, Tagger waved goodbye to everyone as she headed toward town. She always enjoyed the walk through the woods.

Today was exceptionally grand. She didn't remember fall ever being quite so beautiful as it was this year. She loved the deep red, almost magenta leaves of the oaks the best. Soon their leaves would turn—last of the season. The oak was such a noble tree—tall and stately. Two squirrels scampered along the ground among the acorns, busily collecting them for winter.

She could hardly wait until tomorrow night when she and John would go to school together. It would be so exciting to share her learning with her friend. Nothing thrilled Tagger more than learning. She would never be bored as long as there were books to read and facts to learn.

As she sauntered across the square in the direction of John's market, she passed close to a group of shop owners gathered in a tight knot, talking quietly. They didn't notice her, but she happened to overhear some of their conversation. They seemed to be angry over John's success, just as they had been over Gina's.

Tagger pretended not to hear and hurried by. What could they mean, she thought. How could anyone think badly of John? She must have misunderstood.

Tom Derek, the group's leader, frightened her. She

remembered now that once she'd seen him late at night when she was passing by. He was cleaning up his shop. Just as she was even with the storefront, she saw him knock over a large glass jar, full of marinated herring. He was incensed. He'd cursed and yelled loud enough to raise the dead.

His poor, skinny dog came shyly from the back room, cowering, but worried about his owner. Tom saw him and kicked viciously at the animal until he ran howling out into the street. Tagger never respected the man after that and realized how violent he could be.

By the time she reached John's shop, she'd decided not to mention the conversation to him. There was no point in upsetting him needlessly. Perhaps she'd only imagined they were talking about him.

"I have good news, John," Tagger said excitedly as she entered the shop. "Mr. Jensen wants you to come to class with me. We'll have such fun."

"Oh that is good news! Thank you for arranging it, Tagger. When do we start?"

"Tonight," she grinned. "At six o'clock, in the schoolhouse. Mr. Jensen has brought back new books from England, and he's as anxious as we are to start classes."

"Let's celebrate," John suggested. "I'll take you to dine at the Brass Pony."

It took only a few moments to temporarily close up the shop. He hung a sign in the door and gallantly took her arm as they strolled out of the shop.

The group of men was still gathered by the clump of trees near the village courthouse, talking intently. Tagger shivered as they passed by, on the other side of the street. She glanced at John to see if he noticed. He didn't seem to pay the men any attention, but somehow he just wasn't himself today.

The Brass Pony was full of the usual noontime crowd. Some of the diners smiled and even waved at the pair as they searched for a spot to sit. The smell of homemade bread, sugar-cured ham, and pastries floated from the kitchen.

Tagger and John sidled through the diners until they reached a table for two near the window. It was a perfect spot overlooking a long courtyard, where villagers strolled by on their midday dining hour.

John ordered, and Tagger was pleased with his choices— applesauce, roasted beef, and Yorkshire pudding. How she loved the texture of Yorkshire pudding and the way it absorbed the tastes of the meat juices. She'd had it only once before when Gina fixed it for her one night in her apartment above the shop, but she remembered it well.

They discussed the lessons he'd soon be having, and then Tagger began telling him about a book she'd just read on Sir Isaac Newton. Just as she was finishing, the serving girl returned with a steaming tray of food.

The tastefully prepared food warmed her and gave her a mellow feeling. John's attentive eyes made her glow too. Moments like this should last forever, she thought.

CHAPTER 33
The Dedication

The afternoon of the big day was overcast and dreary, but no one seemed to notice. It was moving day, and everyone was ready. Renaud and Diane worked tirelessly on the pier, loading nets and lines and bait buckets into one of the fish carts. They would have to roll it to the warehouse several times to transport everything from the pier. But no one complained. Edward seemed happy too as he lugged *Determined*'s extra sails and fittings up from the beach, stumbling over the coiled lines.

Next they all began to meticulously gather up the fishing hooks of various sizes, which were scattered all over the pier. At first they tried to sort them by size and put them into separate little boxes. Finally they just shrugged at each other, laughing, and started tossing them all into a small metal pail. "We'll sort them later," they said in unison.

Everyone had noticed Mary's absence on moving day. There was no question that Mary was a hard-working and dependable employee, but sometimes she wouldn't come to work. They were afraid she was sick on those days, but she never let on if she was. She always worked twice as hard the next day to make up for the lost day. There were so many questions about the older woman. They didn't know if she had any family, where she lived or what had happened to her that made her so guarded.

Tagger was closer to Mary than anyone, but even she admitted she knew little about her. She had respected Mary's privacy. She never mentioned her growing sight problem either, because she knew it bothered her a great deal. Their friendship had grown stronger because Tagger had not pried. Once she thought she should offer to buy Mary spectacles, but she knew what her answer would be, "Too expensive! I can take care of myself."

Diane and Renaud brought a loaded cart up to the entrance of the warehouse where Tagger was waiting to welcome them. She showed them where to dump their load.

"Come, look what I had built over here," Tagger beamed. They followed her, looking around their new surroundings, trying to take it all in, glad to be out of the brisk wind.

She took them around the corner of the storage area, up three wooden steps and through a door. Inside, the room was warm and cozy. There was a table with a cloth cover, chairs, a wood stove in the corner, an ice box, a little wash bowl and books stacked on one end of the table with a kerosene lamp on it. Coffee steamed on the stove.

Before Renaud and Diane could say anything, Tagger poured them each a cup of coffee. She passed one to Diane and then Renaud, watching their expressions.

"Tagger," Diane smiled slowly after she'd taken it all in, "how thoughtful of you! Our own little room for noonday dinner."

Before the Fish Children left, she told them she had planned a celebration for four o'clock. Everyone agreed to help each other, so they could finish up before then.

She was all alone now. Hank and Patrick were done, although she'd invited them back for the dedication. They'd enjoyed the work so much, they hesitated to charge Tagger the full price for the project. But she insisted on paying them handsomely.

Tagger was clear on this point. "You should expect good payment whenever you've done a good job. It's a fair rule. Everybody benefits. Pay should always be based on the quality of the work, not on the ability of the person to pay.

"You also set an excellent example for others when you do your best," Tagger continued. "If your competitors expect the same or better pay, then they must produce the same or better quality. It's such a simple principle, I've never understood why people have such a hard time following it."

Hank and Patrick agreed. They accepted the full payment, because they knew they had built her the best warehouse in this part of Connecticut.

As she stood in the storage area now, sorting the cartload of equipment her crew had brought, she began to think of John. She'd been so busy, she hadn't seen him for a few days. He'd been busy himself with studying.

Just as she'd expected, John loved his lessons. He was nervous at first, afraid he'd appear stupid if he asked too many questions. But soon, he felt comfortable and his probing questions impressed Mr. Jensen. In fact, sometimes Mr. Jensen was hard-put to find an answer for him.

John liked mathematics and the sciences best. They explained many mysteries for him. When Mr. Jensen taught him about the planets and the rotation of the earth around the sun, he was fascinated. It made the universe seem more real to him; it expanded his existence, he told Tagger. He felt that although man seemed so small by comparison, he was in fact so important for his influence over the earth.

They had gone to the Brass Pony after class one night to discuss all of the ideas they had been learning about. Tagger was worried, though. Despite his enthusiasm for school, John was troubled by something—something painful. It showed in his eyes, even when he was smiling.

Then, Tom Derek had strolled into the Brass Pony and headed straight for John. Tagger shuddered. "Well hello, Johnny Boy," Derek said flippantly. "I thought I saw you come in here. Hello miss," he turned and half-smiled at Tagger. Then he looked back at John, and the smile instantly disappeared. "Given any thought to our discussion tonight, John?"

John was tense. "I don't think this is the time to discuss it. I'll talk to you and the others tomorrow."

"I need an answer tonight, Johnny Boy." Derek had been insistent, and his hostility was evident.

"Then I guess the answer is no," John had stated, looking squarely into his adversary's face.

Derek stared back, his mouth set in an ugly twist. Finally he rose and said, between gritted teeth, "I think you'll regret that decision." He tipped his hat to Tagger and stomped out.

Now, with the dedication only a few minutes away, Tagger wondered if John would be here as he'd promised. The party was ready. Tagger had brought sliced turkey, thick bread, apples, oatmeal cookies, and cold, tangy cider. A fresh pot of coffee perked merrily on the wood stove.

Promptly at four o'clock, she called the group together and told them to help themselves. Plates were quickly stacked with food, cups were filled with coffee or cider and everyone ate heartily. Hank and Patrick arrived and seemed to mix comfortably with Tagger's employees. Soon they were all discussing the merits of the warehouse, the shelves which weren't too low, the pegs and drawers for storing small things, the separate partitions.

When Tagger was sure everyone had eaten all he or she could hold, she invited them outside for the little ceremony. They brought their cider or coffee cups and formed a semicircle around Tagger in front of the entrance.

"My dear friends," she started, "I wanted to make this a special occasion, on the day of the opening of our new warehouse. We've come a long way in a short time, and we should be proud." She paused and looked around at the familiar faces and suddenly saw Mary. She had come to join the celebration. Her face was drawn and pale, but she smiled fondly at Tagger.

Relieved, Tagger continued, "I'd like to dedicate this warehouse to all of you. To Mary, Diane, Renaud, and Edward for your hard work over the years, and to Hank and Patrick for building this dream come true." With that, she pulled a rope that caused a sheet to drop away from a beautifully carved sign about ten feet long and three feet high above the door. In bright red letters, it proudly announced: *Spindrift Company*.

Tagger lingered awhile after everyone was gone. She cleaned up the cups and dishes and stacked them in the little cupboard over the stove, and then she checked to make sure the windows were closed and latched.

She couldn't help but wonder why John hadn't come.

Perhaps he had another meeting, or maybe he'd gotten busy just before closing time. John was very thoughtful; he wouldn't have forgotten anything so important to her.

She was locking the heavy entrance door, ready to go home for the night, when she heard someone running up. She froze; she knew something was wrong.

It was Renaud. He'd run all the way back from town to get her. "John's shop . . . his store is on fire. The fire brigade is already there, but they're having trouble putting out the blaze."

Tagger grabbed Renaud's hand, and they rushed down the path toward town.

CHAPTER 34
The Fire

Orange streaks of flames shot from John's butcher shop into the sky and illuminated the black night. Even though she knew what to expect, Tagger was shocked by the inferno. She could feel the heat radiating from the burning storefront when she was more than a hundred yards away.

The firemen had formed a bucket brigade, and many of the villagers had joined the line. They were passing water as quickly as they could, using a dozen or so buckets, drawing water from a tank that horses had pulled to the site.

Where was John? Then, in the bright light of the fire, she spotted him. He was at the head of the line of the bucket brigade, pouring the pitifully small amounts of water onto the menacing flames.

Without hesitation, Tagger ran up to the bucket line to help, but a huge townsman with smudged and sweating cheeks grabbed her and said gently, "This is no place for you, Miss. You'll just slow us up. We need strong men to deal with this monster."

Before she could speak, Renaud stepped up and took her place. Tagger smiled her thanks and ran to see if John needed her. But again another fireman stopped her, and she was forced to stand back with the rest of the ladies in the crowd.

She looked around nervously, hoping for some solution. Suddenly she noticed some male members of the Mystic

River community just standing together in a little group watching, but making no effort to help.

With a sinking feeling, she recognized the same men she had seen in the town square that day, talking about John: Tom Derek, Sam Tipkin, and Douglas Riverton. She studied their expressions; there was no indication of sympathy, no gesture of compassion. Tagger suspected the worst.

Mr. Riverton walked over to Tagger when Derek and Tipkin moved away through the crowd. He talked quickly, constantly looking in the direction of the other two men. Tagger listened intently, while she watched the blaze.

The fire had spread down into the back of the shop now, the smoke billowing from the storefront windows, which had been blown out under pressure from the heat. But it was not the store that Tagger was concerned about.

Behind the store was a shed. This was the place where John kept his extra supplies, equipment and gallons of whale oil for his lights and for lubricating the equipment. And the blasting powder! Tagger remembered the day John had told her that Brent Magrew, a local contractor, had rented space in his shed to store blasting powder for a large construction project.

Suddenly the long flames shot across the short distance to the shed, scorching the fall leaves and dried grass in its path. Tagger was rooted to the ground, paralyzed by fear.

She was the only one who saw him. John was running towards the shed, his face a mask of terror. His unbuttoned jacket flapped in the wind, nearly hiding his one and only weapon to combat the fire—his small bucket. He had to shield his eyes as he ran, to protect them from the heat and smoke that poured from the shop.

The burning timbers from the second floor of the shop

moved and creaked. There was a roaring explosion as they split from the main structure. One large beam held firm, wedged against another timber. But a third, flaming beam, which had stood suspended in air for a few seconds, suddenly began its terrible descent through the black sky. John was running right into its path.

Tagger screamed over and over, "John, come back, a beam is falling!" But he didn't hear her. She was frantic; there was no one near her to help.

She had no choice. She raced past the bucket brigade to John. Everyone saw her, but they were too slow to react. The flaming beam had fallen on John and knocked him to the ground. With a strength she'd never known before, she grabbed the beam and lifted it from the back of his neck. As others ran up to help her, she felt the searing pain in the palms of her hands.

Quickly, they carried John away from the shed. A moment later a huge explosion rocked the village of Portersville, destroying everything John owned.

The wagon ride up to Dr. Smith's house at Head of the River was a long one. Dr. Smith maintained a small infirmary in the two rooms at the rear of his house, and here he took care of patients who required constant attention, like John.

The doctor had sent his wife, Virginia, to accompany the patient in the wagon. Tagger watched John for any sign of movement. She pleaded with Virginia to help him, but all she could do was keep him warm. She did rub ointment on his now scarlet and purple-colored neck and shoulders, but John didn't react at all when it was applied. He was unconscious.

Tagger was afraid John's neck had been broken, but Virginia assured her that it wasn't.

When they finally arrived at Dr. Smith's house, they whisked John and Tagger off to the back rooms. Virginia treated Tagger's burns in one room while Dr. Smith tended to John. Tagger was in agony and despair, but not from her own pain. She was afraid she would never see John conscious again.

As soon as her hands were bandaged, she begged the nurse to let her see John. He was perfectly still and lay on a cot on his stomach with white sheets up to his chin. His head was bandaged and his eyes were closed. Dr. Smith turned as they entered.

"Are you a family member?" the physician asked.

"No, John has no family, but we're close friends," Tagger replied. "My name is Tagger."

"I'm Dr. Smith," he said, nodding solemnly. "Are you the young lady who saved this young man from the explosion? I've heard about what you did. They said you may have saved his life."

Tagger ignored all this. She just wanted to know if John was going to live. "Doctor, will he be all right? How badly is he injured?"

"He has serious burns on his neck and shoulder, and he's still unconscious. I wasn't able to bring him to. When you're better, you can help him, though. Just talk to him. Maybe eventually he'll hear you and regain consciousness. I've done all I can do. Now we have to rely on his will to live. Stand by him; he needs you to pull him through, Tagger."

CHAPTER 35
The Cause

A musty smell drifted out when Tagger swung open the wooden door of her cottage. She left it ajar awhile to air it out. It was good to be in familiar surroundings. She sat down heavily at her small wooden table, glad she could rest for a while.

So much had happened. She thought about the dreadful night when John's shop was burning, and about how frightened she was when the burning timber fell. Then the long hours at Dr. Smith's while she helped care for John, and the even longer hours when she tried to sleep on the soldier's cot in his room.

The Fish Children had helped break the monotony while she waited for John to come to. They stopped by at various times to tell her that all was going well on the pier, except that Mary wasn't there much, and when she was, she didn't seem to have any energy.

A cool, brisk breeze was blowing through the open door now. She shivered slightly, but was reluctant to close the door because the setting sun cheered her ever so slightly.

Memories of the night of the fire were coming to her in a flood now, memories of events she'd almost forgotten. Douglas Riverton had talked to her that night just before the beam had fallen on John; he'd said some alarming words. Mr.

Derek and Mr. Tipkin had tried to force John to do something he didn't want to do. Evidently when he wouldn't cooperate, they'd gotten even. Someone had set the fire, she was sure of it.

Tagger didn't know what to do, but she knew she had to do something—tell somebody. It was her responsibility. She remembered the cold, smug looks on the faces of Tom Derek and Sam Tipkin when they stood watching John's shop burn.

They had to be stopped before they hurt someone else. But she was afraid. Douglas Riverton had warned her that they were a mean lot. Meanness had never stopped her before.

As Tagger waited for sleep that night she resolved to visit Sheriff Anderson tomorrow. She would tell him the things she'd heard before and during the fire. This decision made, she fell into a deep, exhausted sleep.

When she awoke, Tagger had only one thought on her mind—to get to Dr. Smith's. Maybe John had come to, maybe he needed her. But she realized there were other responsibilities she must attend to first.

She brought in water and bathed quickly. She felt invigorated as she dressed in a blue skirt, white cotton blouse and wool jacket.

Having made her decision the night before to contact the sheriff, she had some peace of mind. She still feared John's enemies, but she knew she had to be strong and believe that justice was on her side.

Her steps were firm as she walked the distance to the crossroads. Even though she was eager to address the matters at hand, she knew she had to go to the warehouse first at noon when the Fish Children arrived. Her employees were important too, and she needed to let them know she was all right. "Has anyone heard why the fire started?" Tagger asked her crew as they all clustered around her.

Edward was grim. "They think someone may have started it. They found burnt matches and a scorched, twisted rag near a barrel of turpentine in John's back room. No one knows why anyone would have done it. John was well liked in the village."

Tagger knew that wasn't entirely true, but she didn't want to bring it up now. Instead she said, "Is the sheriff investigating the fire?" She realized she was holding her breath, waiting for an answer.

"Yes, I think so," Renaud offered. "I saw him at the site of the fire. And then I heard he was asking some of the other shop owners if they'd seen anything. When I was at the market, I overhead Sam Tipkin telling a customer that the sheriff had been questioning him."

"Had he seen anything?" Tagger had to know, but she was almost afraid of the answer.

"No, he told the customer he hadn't," Renaud replied, "but somehow I don't think he was telling the whole story. He didn't sound very convincing."

CHAPTER 36
The Report

Before she left the Fish Children at Spindrift Company, Tagger gave them detailed instructions for operating the business and asked them to help her out just a while longer. They readily agreed and told her to take care of herself. She left the pier and headed directly to Sheriff Anderson's office.

The sheriff saw her coming and went out to greet her. He wanted to know about John and was sorry to hear that he had not regained consciousness. And then he saw Tagger's bandaged hands.

"Oh Tagger, I didn't know you were injured too. Why didn't you tell me? Are you all right?"

"I'm fine." Then she blurted out her message, the one she'd rehearsed. "I have information which might help you find out who burned down John Garth's shop."

The constable plopped down in his chair, surprised by the turn of events, "What makes you think someone did it?"

Tagger wasn't prepared for that response; she hesitated briefly. And then, she told him the whole story: the men gathered in the square; the threats made by Tom Derek and the disinterested shop owners who watched John's store burn.

"I'm afraid that's not much to go on, Tagger. There's no law against a fellow talking bad about another fellow. Maybe some of the villagers just don't like Garth. He is new in town, and he stays pretty much to himself. Folks just get a little put off by newcomers sometimes, especially when they do well. Folks are just a little jealous, I'd say."

Tagger considered his words for a moment. Of course he was right. She hadn't really given him much substantial evidence of a crime. She would have to tell him what she'd heard from Douglas Riverton. She'd been avoiding that, reluctant to betray his confidence.

Before she could go on, there was a knock at the door of the office. The sheriff opened the door to Douglas Riverton. He held his gray, felt hat loosely in his hand and stared down at it for a moment, summoning his courage to speak. When he looked up, he was surprised to see Tagger there and nodded nervously.

"I want to report some information I have about the fire at John Garth's." He said it in a strong voice. Still, his lower lip trembled a bit as he spoke. "All I can tell you is that there was a meeting about a month ago above Tom Derek's store. Four of the Mystic River area butcher shop owners were there: Tom Derek, Sam Tipkin, myself and John Garth. Tom and Sam insisted that Garth come, and he agreed, but said he didn't really like that type of thing."

Riverton continued, braver now that he had the sheriff's attention. "Tom and Sam called the meeting because they wanted to threaten Garth into fixing his prices. They were losing money because he was charging less for meat and seafood than they were, and they said they couldn't compete. They wanted support from me too, but I didn't say much during the meeting."

"Well, what happened?" Sheriff Anderson boomed. "Get on with your story."

"Please, give me a chance, sir," Riverton pleaded. "This isn't easy for me." He paused slightly, caught his breath and continued. "Garth didn't like what he was hearing, but he was trying to be a gentleman and at least listen to their proposal. When the time came to say whether or not he would agree, he told Derek he would give them an answer later. They threatened to bring harm to John and his store unless he agreed. Evidently Garth told them later he wouldn't agree to raise his prices. On the evening of the fire, just before it started, I saw Derek and Tipkin slipping out the back door of Garth's shop."

Sheriff Anderson stared at them both for a moment in quiet thought and then he shrugged. "Well, I guess I'd better arrest Tom Derek and Sam Tipkin and bring them in for questioning. Are both of you prepared to give this testimony when those two are brought before the magistrate?"

Tagger and Riverton nodded silently. "And Tagger," the sheriff said softly, "I hope John will be able to join you to substantiate what you've both told me today."

"Thank you, sir. I hope he'll be there too."

CHAPTER 37
The Awakening

By the time she reached Dr. Smith's, the afternoon sun was sinking in the west. It cast long shadows on the stone walkway as she walked quickly to John's room.

Dr. Smith was just coming out when she approached. He looked somber as he rubbed his white beard.

Tagger ran to him. "Oh Doctor, is he worse?"

"No, dear, he's the same, but it's time he should be coming to. I'm worried that if he doesn't come around soon, there may be permanent damage."

The words crushed her. "I've tried so hard to get through to him, but he just doesn't hear me. He's so still, it's as though he's left his body and gone to another place."

Dr. Smith left, and Tagger sat beside John as the twilight darkened the room. She was so intent upon watching him that she barely noticed when Virginia came in to light the lamps. She asked Tagger if she was hungry, but she shook her head dismally.

When night settled in, Tagger knew she would have to go soon. Renaud would be there in half an hour to walk her home. As Tagger moved to leave, she grasped John's hand and said in a tense, determined voice, "John, you must come back to me—I care so much for you!" Silence. His serene face lay perfectly still. She could barely see his chest moving as he breathed.

And then as she started to rise, in despair, she thought she noticed a slight twitching at the corner of John's mouth. It was almost like the tiny smile he'd try to hide when he thought she was being funny and she wasn't.

And then she saw his hand move. There was no mistaking it now; he was reaching toward her. Slowly, he opened his eyelids, battling the deep sleep that had held him in its clutches for so long.

Tagger let out a gasp for joy. When he had fully regained consciousness and drank the large glass of water that Tagger brought him, he began asking the many questions that would help him catch up on all the events since the night of the fire.

"Tagger, you saved my life," he exclaimed after she'd told him that she'd pulled the burning beam off his neck. "Let me see your hands."

When she held up her hands, he could see that long dark, purplish scars were forming where the skin was beginning to heal. He knew how they must feel, because the same pain was spreading across his neck and shoulders now.

"No one has ever cared enough about me to make that kind of sacrifice. You are truly an angel." He looked at her lovingly.

"John, when you're well enough to leave the doctor's house, Renaud has volunteered to let you stay with him until you either rebuild your store or find another job. We'll help you until you're on your feet."

"Tagger, I'll be fine. I've saved some money for emergencies, and it's at the bank in town."

She smiled. "I knew you would never let anyone help you.

They're going to arrest the cruel and selfish men who started the fire. They should be made to rebuild the shop. You should have told me—or someone—they were threatening you."

"Yes, I suppose you're right. I never thought they would go that far."

John looked at Tagger silently for some time, taking in every aspect of her face and eyes and hair. "Tagger, you mean the world to me. My whole life changed when you came into it. We were meant to be together. Will you to marry me as soon as I'm well? We can rebuild together. We're young, but we're both mature, and we've been through so much. We deserve some happiness now. Please say you'll marry me."

Tagger didn't hesitate, "Yes, John, of course I'll marry you." Tears of joy welled up in her eyes as she leaned over to kiss him. "I've loved you for so long."

Later, Tagger sat at her table recalling all this, she realized she now had good news for all her friends.

CHAPTER 38
The Heroes

When Renaud met Tagger on the path to Head of the River, she told him the news of the wedding to come. She hadn't planned to tell anyone yet, but she just couldn't wait to share the news.

"Tagger, I guess I'd always hoped you and I would marry someday, but John is a perfect match for you. You two will be very happy together."

As they continued to walk to Dr. Smith's, Tagger looked at Renaud and saw that something else was wrong. "What is it, Renaud? Something's troubling you."

"Tagger, I'm so sorry. While I was at Dr. Smith's earlier talking with John, they brought someone else in. I didn't recognize her at first, she was so white and frail." He paused here, and Tagger nearly went wild with worry.

"Who was it, Renaud?"

"It was Mary. She was unconscious when she arrived, but she came to after they put her in the room. Dr. Smith doesn't know what's wrong with her, yet."

They walked along in silence again; Tagger had so much to think about. She could barely wait to get to Dr. Smith's.

When they came over the hill, they could see that a crowd was gathering near the doctor's gate. The villagers separated as Tagger and Renaud passed by, and everyone smiled and patted her on the back. She was puzzled, but guessed they were just being friendly. Maybe it was some sort of village meeting, but she noticed that people from both sides of the river had gathered here.

Tagger hurried to the room next to John's and peeked in. Another woman she didn't know was slowly covering up the slight figure in the bed. "Oh, no," Tagger gasped. "Mary's not, not . . ."

"No, no," the nurse whispered, turning now to face Tagger. "She's just resting. The doctor has given her laudanum to make her sleep."

"Is she going to be all right?" Tagger wondered.

The woman steered Tagger out of the door, tapping her forefinger against her pursed lips. "Let's let her sleep now," she whispered.

When they were outside, she introduced herself as Julia McKown. Tagger started to introduce herself, but Julia said, "Oh I know who you are, dear. Mary has spoken often of you. I've known her for a long time, and she's told me about your business and what you've done for the orphan children in town."

"Mary's a good friend." Tagger said.

Julia told Tagger that she had been a neighbor of Mary's at one time, and they had been friends, but they'd lost touch over the years, when Mary moved. Julia was Dr. Smith's cousin and sometimes helped out with patients. She had found her old friend again when Mary had come in to see the doctor a couple of years ago.

"Dr. Smith examined her thoroughly today," she said, "but he can't seem to find out what's wrong. He's guarded about her condition. Tagger, I know you're here to take John home, but if you'd like to come back later, we can talk about Mary if you'd like."

"Yes, I'd like that. I'll be back as soon as we have John settled in."

When Tagger went to John's room, he was ready to go. Extra clothing that Tagger had brought him was packed in a small black carpet bag. He said Dr. Smith had come and gone and had told him he was doing fine. He could leave now. Was he ever glad! He asked about Mary, and Tagger told him briefly about her conversation with Julia.

Tagger took the bag and Renaud helped John to his feet. They began to walk with John leaning heavily on Renaud. Virginia followed them out, giving them last-minute instructions for caring for John. As they passed Mary's room, Tagger peeped in for a moment. She saw that Mary was still resting quietly, small and pale under the white sheets and blanket.

When the small procession reached the door, Renaud stepped ahead to open it. Then he stopped for a moment and stared out.

"What is it, Renaud?" John asked, seeing the surprise on Renaud's face.

"I'm not sure," the young man mused. "I think it's some kind of celebration—for you and Tagger."

Renaud was right. When they stepped out on the porch, they saw most of the villagers from the Mystic River community, on the road or in the Doctor's yard, cheering, waving placards. The good doctor was among them. They'd come to honor John and Tagger.

A distinguished older gentleman with thick white hair, loped up the steps as soon as he saw the trio emerge. It was

James Sherman, the selectman from Portersville. He helped John to a wooden chair on the doctor's front porch.

"As you all know, we're gathered here today to honor John Garth and Miss Tagger." The crowd roared in unison. "Both are heroes in Mystic. Mr. Garth had the courage to say no to corruption. He had the strength that comes to someone when he is in the right.

"Mr. Garth hasn't been in Portersville long," he continued, "but in the short time since he opened his store, he's brought us good meat and fish at fair prices. But what's more important, he's withstood the pressure from some weak people in our community who wanted to cheat the public.

"We know what you've gone through because of your convictions, John, and now we want to show you our appreciation. The villagers of Portersville, Head of the River, Noank, and Mystic Bridge are going to rebuild your store. It will be a labor of love for us, and it will give us a chance to show you that we're not like the evil men who started the fire."

The crowd cheered. When the noise died down finally, John spoke from the heart. "I'm proud to be a part of this community. But what I want most is for you to use your labor to build an orphanage for the Mystic River area. There are orphanages—homes for homeless children—in places like New York and New Orleans already. We should have one here. That way, children without parents, like Tagger and me, will have a good start in life. And as soon as I'm well, I'd like to help too."

After the applause died down again, Mr. Sherman said, "That's very generous of you, Mr. Garth, We'll do just that, and we'll name it in your honor."

And now it was Tagger's turn. "Miss Tagger, your courage

has not gone unnoticed either. You have accomplished much at a very young age. Not only have you started a modern business and employed many people in the area, you've also demonstrated your ability to think quickly during an emergency. We know that if it hadn't have been for you, Mr. Garth wouldn't be here today. In honor of your heroism, I'd like to present you with this key to the Mystic River villages."

Tagger stepped forward to receive the large, gold key on the wide blue ribbon. The selectman shook her hand warmly and smiled down at her as the people cheered and applauded.

"Thank you, my friends," she started shakily. "This is quite an honor. I don't feel I did anything the rest of you wouldn't have done in the same circumstances. It's natural to help someone in trouble. But I'll treasure this key forever and the love you've shown us today."

After the applause subsided, John quieted them completely by holding up his hands. Tagger knew his burns hurt him, but they were both so elated by the gratitude of the town, they seemed to be moving in a dream.

When all was still, John said, "We were waiting for the proper moment to make this announcement, but since all our friends are here now, this seems as good a time as any. I've asked Tagger to be my wife, and she's accepted. We're planning a May wedding, and you're all invited."

Everyone started crowding the steps now to shake John's hand and hug Tagger. This was a moment the Mystic River community would never forget.

Tagger could see the warmth and love in the faces of the people as they crowded around her. There was Betty who was still running the lodging house with the aid of her daughter— she had helped Tagger so long ago. And Sheriff and Mrs.

Anderson, the Fish Children, Mr. Riverton and Harold Evings from the Unitarian Church. And best of all, Mr. Jensen the schoolmaster.

A liveried coach, trimmed in dark carved wood, with two coachmen, drew up in front of the doctor's house, and Mr. Sherman himself helped John into it. After he'd been lifted in, Tagger and Renaud climbed in behind him and they moved off through the crowd.

CHAPTER 39
The Past

Tagger had never seen Renaud's room in the blacksmith's shop before. When he had finished his service with the blacksmith, he'd taken responsibility for the shop and the aging smithy who had employed him. Edward had done the same at the livery stable. Both of these gentle Fish Children were far kinder to their masters than their masters had been to them. Renaud's room was small, but comfortable, and he had all that he needed, including a little kitchen and cupboards stocked with food. It would be a fine place for John to recuperate.

She and Renaud helped John to Renaud's bed and covered him with a blue, handmade quilt. Renaud was such a good friend; he would sleep on the settee in the little parlor until John was ready to find his own place. She kissed John lightly on the lips and hugged Renaud. They all knew it was time for her to meet Julia McKown.

When she returned to Dr. Smith's, Julia was waiting for Tagger. Mary was still sleeping, so they went into the room that John had just vacated.

Julia was a tall woman, about thirty or thirty-five with light brown hair, which she wore wound up in a knot on her head. Her warm, brown eyes were deep set and her mouth curved up gently. Tagger liked her as soon as they had met.

She smiled when she saw Tagger. "I'm so glad you came. You need to know about Mary, and then perhaps you can help."

"Of course, I'll try," Tagger said, as she settled into the chair opposite Julia at a small wooden table. She sipped the strong coffee that Julia had brought her and waited attentively.

"Well," Julia began, "I think Mary is very ill, but not with any disease the doctor can fix. I think she's dying of a broken heart."

Tagger's eyes widened. "What do you mean?"

"In reality, she's probably ill from not eating properly, from working too hard and from too much exposure to the elements. But I know it's all because her heart aches so much that she doesn't have the will to live anymore."

"Oh," Tagger murmured solemnly, "poor Mary. Do you know why she's so sad?"

"Yes, I think so," Julia replied. "I haven't seen much of Mary recently, but long ago, my family and hers were neighbors. I was friends with her daughter."

Tagger showed surprise. "I didn't know she had a daughter. Where is she? Has she come to see her mother?"

"No, I'm afraid not. Let me explain." The good woman was obviously struggling to find the right words, and Tagger sensed there was much more to Mary's life than she had realized.

"Mary and her husband, Richard, were both fishermen," Julia started. "They were poor, but they managed to eke out a living. They had a little house next to ours on Mistuxet Avenue in Mystic Bridge. When Mary was in her late thirties, she became pregnant. Although she and Richard were thrilled about the baby, they worried that they didn't have enough money to care for it properly.

"Richard was much older than Mary, but he took another job, working on one of the sailing packets that delivered goods up and down the eastern shoreline. He made a great deal more money at that job, but the work was hard, especially during the winter months.

"Their baby daughter was born in the spring, and Mary and Richard were joyous. They spoiled her with everything they could afford. She had dolls and playhouses and the prettiest clothes you've ever seen. I know, because she and I were about the same age, and we went to school together. I used to be a little envious of her, because she had the best of everything, and yet everyone loved her because she was so sweet.

"And then life went sour for them. Richard got sick—consumption. He had to quit his job, and Mary had to take care of the family, doing the only thing she knew, fishing. Richard's condition worsened, and then, right after their daughter's sixteenth birthday, he died.

"Mary and her daughter were heartbroken for months. Finally, Mary realized she was responsible for keeping their lives together, and she went back to work. But the meager money she made as a fisherwoman barely kept food in the house; and she had nothing left to pay the medical bills.

"Mary had no choice; she had to tell her daughter she would have to quit school and go to work. It was terrible for Mary's daughter to leave school and her friends. But she did as she was told. She found employment sewing sails at the Blanchard sail loft. Her pay was adequate, but she had to work long hours and there was no time for friends.

"Her daughter became more and more despondent, and soon she went from being a bubbly young girl to a quiet and sullen young woman. Then to Mary's great disappointment, she began spending time with a no-good young sailor who came into port on occasion. But she seemed to enjoy his company, so Mary didn't try to stop her.

"All Mary's fears were realized. The sailor got her daughter pregnant and when he found out, he said the baby was her problem, not his. That was the last time he was ever seen in the Mystic River area.

"Her daughter didn't want the baby, but she had no choice. She didn't think she and Mary could afford to raise her, but she couldn't find anyone to take her. When the baby was born, she was beautiful, and Mary fell in love with her immediately. She had curly, dark brown hair and big blue eyes.

"Such a sad situation. Mary idolized her granddaughter, but had nothing to give her—nothing but love. They barely managed to live. Her daughter grew more and more bitter; she knew she'd never find a proper husband now that she had a baby in tow.

"One day, in the late fall, when the granddaughter was five, Mary woke up and found that they were both gone. There was a note, but it didn't say much—something like, 'Mama, I couldn't stay in this town anymore. There's nothing here for me. I'm going down the coast and take a ship to a place where I can start my life over again.'

"Her daughter had taken all of her clothes, but she took only a few of her granddaughter's. Mary and her friends searched everywhere, and then they finally learned her daughter had booked passage in Providence on a ship bound for London. To Mary's shock, she learned she hadn't purchased a ticket for the granddaughter—nothing could be learned of her.

"Mary became deeply melancholy. Many of her friends thought she would die then, but she was a strong lady. Gradually she began to work again to keep herself alive, but she was never the same. You were good for her, Tagger. When she started helping you with your business, I saw her come back to life a bit. You seemed to give her a reason to live again."

"I'm so glad," Tagger answered, "I guess she needed us as much as we needed her. Why has she gotten worse recently?"

"Well something happened," Julia replied. "Mary received a letter recently from her daughter. She's older now, and I guess she finally felt some remorse for the daughter she left behind. Apparently she told Mary the truth—that she'd left her granddaughter with a friend who had actually paid for her. That was where she got the money to go to England.

"Mary was devastated. She realized finally that she'd lost her daughter and would never again see her granddaughter. It was a cruel thing to do; Mary's much older now and doesn't have the strength to fight for life the way she used to."

Tagger sat quietly staring at the nurse. "Oh what a sad story. Poor Mary. What can I do to help her?"

"Just be her friend. I know she hasn't been eating. I just heard you're getting married; tell her about it. Make her see your joy. I think I hear her stirring. Let's go see if she's awake."

Mary was awake and propped up on pillows when Tagger tiptoed in. Tagger was shocked at how pale she was. Her face was nearly as white as her tangled hair, and her eyes were sunken and swollen. Purple shadows filled the area beneath her half-closed eyelids.

"You shouldn't have come here, Tagger," Mary said, looking up at her with sad, dim eyes. "You must be so busy now with John and the company. I'll be all right. Julia is taking good care of me here."

"I know," Tagger replied as cheerfully as possible, "but we've all been worried about you." Tagger knew she needed to keep talking, needed to be positive. "Did you know that the whole town gathered to honor John when he was released?"

"No, I didn't," Mary answered weakly. "He deserved it, and so do you for saving his life."

"They presented me with a key to the all the villages of the Mystic River," Tagger added. "And the villagers also volunteered to rebuild John's business. He asked them to build an orphanage for the town instead."

With this Mary broke into heart-rending sobs. Tagger rushed to the bed and held Mary in her arms, crying with her. Mary's body was so frail; she could feel her shoulder blades protruding through the skin on her back.

When her crying had subsided, Mary began to talk. Maybe it was the comfort of Tagger's arms around her that made her talk, or maybe the tears had opened the floodgate. She poured out the same story Julia had just told her. Tagger frowned in thought.

"We were so poor when my granddaughter was born," Mary sobbed, "that I couldn't give her anything. The only little toy I had for Elizabeth was an old doorknob, and she would play with it endlessly. I would watch her play with that doorknob, and it would make me cry inside, because I couldn't give her anything better."

Elizabeth? Tagger thought. Wasn't Lizzie a nickname for

Elizabeth? "What did the doorknob look like, Mary?" she whispered.

Mary was surprised by the question and stared at Tagger. "I don't know," she said. "It was just an old brass doorknob, pretty standard, I guess, but it did have an unusual design on it. It had a raised diamond decoration on the front. In the center was a black enamel circle that looked like a piece of ebony, but of course, it was just paint."

"Oval? Was it oval-shaped, Mary?" Tagger scarcely dared to breathe.

"Yes, oval, but why?"

"Oh, Mary, I'm not sure, but I think I played with that doorknob when I was a baby."

"What, oh Tagger, what are you saying?" The color seemed to rise up from Mary's throat, and her eyes widened. "Where did you come from, Tagger? Do you know where you were born?"

"No, I just know I lived in Mystic Bridge before I lived in Groton. My mother took me there and left me with a lady named Miss Devlin. She said she was coming back, but she never came for me."

When she heard the name "Miss Devlin," Mary's eyes widened even more. "Rita Devlin—Rebecca's friend! She lived in Groton."

"Mary, isn't Becky a nickname for Rebecca? And Lizzie, they called me Lizzie. Isn't that a nickname for Elizabeth?" Tagger excitement was growing.

"Yes, oh yes," Mary cried. "You are my dear, sweet Elizabeth, Elizabeth Stuart, born on July 8, 1819." Tagger wrapped her arms around Mary and they cried together.

"Nana, I've found you," Tagger sobbed.

Finally, Tagger brought Mary to the present. "I've been waiting to tell you this, until just the right time. John asked me to marry him in the spring, and I need you to be there with me, to sit in the seat where the bride's mother sits to witness my happiness. I'll have a grandmother and a husband at the same time."

"Elizabeth—Tagger—this has been the most joyous day of my life. Of course, I'll be there."

Maybe some people would have thought it was a strange place to marry, but Elizabeth, John, Mary and the Fish Children thought it made perfect sense. John and Elizabeth were to be married on the sagging, but repaired, pier where "Tagger" had caught her first fish so many years ago.

CHAPTER 40
The Future

It was a typical May day on the sound, sunny and breezy. Nearly everyone from both sides of the Mystic River had come, no longer fearing the pier they'd once thought was cursed. A platform, with risers had been built along the shoreline, facing the sound and the spot where the young couple would soon exchange their vows.

Tagger's veil was simple, but elegant, made of white thin silk, trimmed in delicate lace that flowed out the back to the end of the train of her simple white dress. Around the silk crown of the veil were dozens of small daisies, braided together by their stems. She held a bouquet of larger daisies tied in satin ribbons.

Each person in the bridal party had rehearsed his or her role and knew it well. Diane, who was married now, was Tagger's matron of honor. She stepped off the distance to the pier in perfect measure to the soft violin music played by Douglas Riverton. She turned to the left as she reached the spot where John stood with Renaud and Edward.

Elizabeth followed on the arm of Mr. Jensen. The crowd cheered when they saw Elizabeth, the little girl with the big dreams, for this was their moment too. But when she and Mr. Jensen reached John, a hush fell over the assembly. Only

the sound of gulls, wheeling overhead, sounded the trumpet call of love. Mr. Jensen handed Elizabeth ever so carefully over to John, as she kissed him on the cheek.

Reverend Evings, the Unitarian Minister, conducted the ceremony. He started by saying they were assembled here on this day, at the edge of the ocean, to join together John Garth and Elizabeth Stuart in matrimony. "Who giveth this bride to this man?"

Mary rose and in a clear, melodious voice said, "Her loving grandmother does." There was not a dry eye in the crowd. Mary was strong and healthy now, dressed in the old but beautifully preserved rose dress she'd worn for her own small wedding some fifty years earlier. The new eyeglasses Tagger had bought her sparkled in the sun.

After the ceremony, everyone gathered on the shore where tables had been set up to enjoy the reception. The villagers stood in line to congratulate the couple; it seemed important just to touch the golden children who had changed their lives.

After they'd shared slices of the wedding cake that baker Roy provided, Tagger and John called the group together. "We hope all of you will stop by the site in Portersville where the Mystic River orphanage is being built. You all are a part of that orphanage, and children for years to come will thank you for your kindness."

Then they said their goodbyes and climbed into a waiting carriage. John had made all the plans from here on, so Elizabeth would be totally surprised.

The coachman drove on in silence for awhile as Elizabeth's curiosity grew. Finally, she felt the carriage slow and heard the loud, "Whoa" from the driver.

When he'd helped Elizabeth from the carriage, John

waved the coachmen on, and then led her up a path, lined with rose bushes, to the most beautiful white cottage she'd ever seen. Although darkness had set in, she could see in the moonlight that vines of English ivy climbed the walls beside the door and that the windows were framed with green shutters.

She gasped when she realized this was their new home. John lit a candle he'd brought and wordlessly leaned down to unlock the door. As the candle shown brilliantly in the darkness, she saw it—an oval, brass doorknob with a diamond design and a tiny black circle in the middle.

He turned the doorknob and swept her into his arms. As he carried her across the threshold, he whispered in one ear, while the sound of the ocean roared in the other, "This is the beginning of our new life together, Elizabeth."

She was no longer alone.

About the
Author

The story of Tagger is based on a bedtime tale that J. A. Louthain's father told her as a child. The story took life when Louthain visited Mystic, Connecticut, on her way home from a business trip.

Louthain began her writing career as a magazine article writer while working full-time for the Federal Government. Now retired, she finally found the time to finish the novel. *Tagger* first appeared as an e-book on fatbrain.com and later on mightywords.com where it was on the featured list of children's books for several weeks and was rated four and a half stars by readers.

She is currently working on her next novel, *Raven on the Edge*, an eerie tale that takes place in the deep South and is based upon a true encounter.

Louthain lives part of the year on a quiet pond in Carmel, Indiana, and part of the year on the ocean in Garden City, South Carolina, with her husband, Ron, two parrots, Willy and Shorty, and a cat, Smokie.

Visit J. A. Louthain on the web at www.alexiebooks.com.

About the Illustrator

Nationally known illustrator Andrea Eberbach was designer for the Everett Children's Adventure Garden at the New York Botanical Garden and her work has been published in such magazines as the *Atlantic Monthly, Business Week, Dell Magazine* and *National Marketing*. She has illusrated books for Harcourt Brace Jovanovish, Houghton Mifflin, Little Brown, MacMillan, Scribner and Simon and Schuster.

Eberbach (her married name McCollam) lives with her husband Gregg, son Noah and daughter Erica in Indianapolis, Indiana.